I0568014

Syreen escaped from her prison, but she's still deep in enemy territory. Her enemies are countless, and their master turned out to be one of her own people. Shaken by her findings, she must find a way back to her ship and her few allies, with an entire hostile navy searching for her. Will she be able to cover her tracks better this time?

But the enemy master has a few more tricks up his sleeve.

Time of Wonders
Copyright © 2020 Valerie J. Long
ISBN: 978-1-4874-2935-5
Cover art by Martine Jardin

Published by eXtasy Books Inc or
Devine Destinies, an imprint of eXtasy Books Inc

Look for us online at:
www.eXtasybooks.com or www.devinedestinies.com

TIME OF WONDERS
FORGOTTEN PEOPLE BOOK 3

BY

VALERIE J. LONG

DEDICATION

In memory of the famous Dublin fishmonger, Molly Malone

PART ONE—EVASION

CHAPTER ONE

Two armed MPs came running up the corridor of Nysa Four Space Base Gamma. A quick step to the wall took the young officer out of the Military Police's path before she continued her way to the shuttle bay.

The next centicycles were crucial for Syreen's unhindered departure. Her stolen uniform seemed to itch in all the wrong places. That wouldn't have mattered if her ID was fine—it was, but it was stolen, too.

She turned around the corner and faced the security desk.

The single noncom might've been charmed to let her pass—the ID scanner he carried couldn't be fooled by her looks.

Her timing was perfect, however. The noncom ignored her, only paying attention to Admiral Tas and his entourage. She joined them, smiled, and when Flag Captain Munoz patted her shoulder and said, "Great you made it on time," she ultimately disappeared from the noncom's radar. No AP noncom would dare to delay an admiral on the way to his ship—or, in case he had considered this, a gentle mental push relieved him from any such ambitions.

Perhaps he was distracted, too—the two MPs surely weren't the only ones alerted. The space base buzzed with excitement. She could imagine the reason—someone must have found the corpse of her last victim, the officer whose uniform she was wearing now.

"Come on, the shuttle's waiting," Munoz said.

She followed him to the access tunnel.

1

CHAPTER TWO

I am a Navigator. As far as I know, I'm the last surviving female of my People, the only one capable of controlling a living ship. I know, because I found one.

When I listen, I hear the songs the stars are singing to their planets. I hear their lonesome, never answered lament. Their songs guide me through space, let me find the smoothest way through hyperspace.

My enemies are score, and their master is of my People, too. He is searching for an ancient relic *to give him power over a living ship. He is a male, though, and thus will never command. The* relic *he needs is a female Navigator — that's me, only he doesn't know that yet.*

When he caught me, he regarded me as nothing more than a defiant obstacle, a minor hindrance to his plans. He didn't recognize the reason for my mental resilience. He had me tortured in order to break me. He failed.

I control the minds of the lesser races. I make them ignore me or follow my orders. By feeding on their blood, I gain power or heal my injuries. Such are the ways of my People, and such I did to my torturer, before I left my enemy master's lair.

"Captain Gryf?"

That's me, Captain Ishtar Gryf. That's the name and role I adopted in order to escape Nysa, the Association's home system. The Association, commanded by their master, sent out ships in search for the relic. *They came to my home world, the Duchy, and wiped out our fleet, our orbital stations, our planetary defenses, and every civilian in their way without declaring war. In my eyes, such action*

2

counts as piracy, and thus every single member of their forces is fair game for me.

"Yes, Flag Captain?"

"Would you like to assist Ensign Torres with his jump calculations?"

"Of course."

This is a request I can never reject. I'm a Navigator, and navigating is what I do.

Syreen had to be careful not to give herself away. So she walked over to the navigation dashboard on the battle cruiser's spacious bridge and silently watched the ensign entering his parameters. When he was ready and looked up, she gave him an approving nod. There was no flaw in his setup for this easy jump.

However, when he reached for the button to release his five-sigma solution, she said, "Wait."

He turned to her again with a puzzled face. "Captain?"

"There is no flaw in your solution, Ensign. But why didn't you look for possible refinements? There's no pressing need to jump, as we haven't even reached jump speed yet."

"Uh, what refinements, Captain?"

Syreen had to fight with herself not to roll her eyes. What did the Association teach these young officer candidates?

She wouldn't teach her tricks to the enemy, but she couldn't let such an outrageous lack of knowledge about the most elementary procedures stand. "Recall your parameters."

He did.

"Good. Now call up the trims."

"Trims?"

"That scales symbol, top right."

"Oh — sure."

He tapped it, and a new set of controls appeared.

"See? Now you can adjust your solution. The colors tell you where you can expect improvements. Note that there may be good reasons not to change certain parameters too

3

much, depending on where you want to go, but you can try and compare several settings. Go ahead."

The candidate started to change settings.

"Note how the colors on the other controls change. Some of your changes will offer you more options, others may narrow down good choices — which means it's an overall tighter solution."

Torres nodded and moved a few sliders, shook his head, reset them, and tried others. Only once did she cough slightly, which quickly made him reset his last change.

Syreen patiently watched him pick three variations, compare them, and arrive at one new solution.

"This is better, I'd say."

This time Syreen nodded. "How much better?"

The ensign checked again and blushed. "Oh. Almost a sigma level."

"So."

"Captain Gryf?" Flag Captain Munoz' demanding voice saved the young man from his embarrassment.

Syreen turned around. "Yes, Sir."

"Are you dissatisfied with Torres' solution?"

"No, Sir. We just arrived at a very good result."

"Submit it. I need to check it myself."

"Yes, Sir." She nudged her pupil, and Torres released the refined solution. "You have it, Sir."

The commandant made a grim face and tapped his panel. His eyebrows rose, his lips opened to a silent "oh," and then he smiled.

"Six-sigma, indeed? Who taught you that, Torres?"

The ensign rose. "Captain Gryf did, Sir."

"In just the past five centicycles?"

"Yes, she did, Sir."

"Remarkable. Ensign, you did an excellent job on this. Captain Gryf, I'm grateful for your lesson. Would you assume

4

command for this transit?"

Syreen smiled. "Yes, Sir."

Munoz returned the smile and rose. "I thought so. Take my seat."

CHAPTER THREE

Syreen feigned hesitation when she approached Munoz' chair. He only smiled and took a free seat toward the aft bulkhead. From there he'd be able to observe her actions—and more, should he feel the need to interfere. Currently, she sensed, he didn't plan to do so.

A pity they're so nice. They're still enemy and I might have to kill them eventually.

As an ordinary Duchy officer, she wouldn't have known the Association's obligatory procedures, but aboard *Raydancer,* her captured AP corvette, she had studied their rules and regulations, so she knew exactly what to do.

She checked all stations at her desk first—surveillance, communications, weapons, navigation, engine—before asking the responsible officers or officer candidates for their reports. Only then did she approve the jump solution.

"Communications, submit to battle group and request acknowledgment."

"Yes, Sir."

The com op watched his panel. "Four acknowledgments, Sir. And I have incoming praises."

"Forward those to navigation, command, and steward. Reconfirm jump." She switched the channel. "Crew, prepare for transit in fifteen."

There was still enough time, so she rechecked the parameters, as Munoz probably would have done, too. Otherwise, she radiated confidence.

Finally, she announced, "Ready for transit in five."

6

Her senses had already picked up the hyperplane's familiar song when the com op said, "Incoming transmission."

The ship jumped.

CHAPTER FOUR

"Fine jump," Munoz said.

Syreen nodded. Yes, it had been a fine jump, six-sigma, excellent by all interstellar standards. Only a Navigator could know that it wasn't the best possible solution, that seven-sigma was possible after some programming enhancements.

Which she wouldn't tell them.

"Fine jump," she echoed. "Thank you, Ensign Torres, and keep up the good work."

"There was a message," the flag captain said. "I'd like to review it—if it won't inconvenience you, I'll withdraw to my office and leave the bridge to you."

"Of course."

With another nod, the commandant left.

Syreen leaned back into her seat and opened her mind for the emotions around her. There was anxiety, excitement, hunger, lust, suppressed violence. Where was this vessel heading to, what were the orders? Was she supposed to know?

She was just a guest on this ship. But now she had assumed command, and unlike other bridge officers and candidates, she wore the stripes of a captain. Thus she was entitled to check at least the basic orders.

Should someone ask, it's a need to know for my secret mission.

The same reasoning applied to a sneak peek into that message, but the computer would record her access—would it?

No. It would record Munoz' access, as he was the one still logged into her panel. It couldn't have worked otherwise, as she didn't have any credentials for the ship's systems.

8

So she checked the message first. It told of a security incident on Nysa Four—a corpse found, identified as Captain Ishtvan Gryf. Evidence suggested a violent death and thus a murderer on the loose. Any recently departed ships should check for suspicious crew activities or blind passengers.

Not good.

She wasn't a blind passenger for sure, but Munoz couldn't fail to notice the striking similarity of the names Ishtvan Gryf and Ishtar Gryf—something that required a very convincing explanation.

If there's one thing besides navigation I'm good at, it's convincing. He'll only have to give me time for explaining — if necessary, I'll make him listen to me.

Her fingers casually moved across the panel, producing the corps' mission orders. The *Oppression* and her escorts were bound for Brannock to establish an example, after a thorough investigation had produced sufficient evidence for the local militia's lack of cooperation. So basically, this was about bullying—or worse.

A navy that wouldn't stop at shooting down orbital stations full of civilians without warning, what would they consider an example? Syreen wouldn't want to know.

Brannock wasn't her business, but this ship's crew was. Meanwhile, she could sense Munoz' rising worries. She'd have to do something about him soon.

Am I already strong enough again?

No.

A pity.

CHAPTER FIVE

Syreen offered no resistance when Munoz returned to the bridge with two armed guards in his wake to arrest her, not even when they applied their handcuffs.

"I'm sorry," the flag captain said. It was a lie.

He wasn't sorry at all, but determined to get rid of her.

Ensign Torres was sorry and confused, but wouldn't dare to speak up in her favor. That wasn't brave but probably wise.

"Put her under arrest. Admiral Tas will deal with her case later."

Another lie. She wasn't meant to see the admiral at all. But when one of them waved her forward with his shock baton, she nodded, smiled and walked off.

They directed her through empty corridors, straight toward the outer hull. Spacing her would be a cheap, clean and final solution for sure—they couldn't know they'd thus deprive their master of his precious *relic*.

He'd be mad, and she'd be dead.

Won't happen.

When they reached the main airlock's inside door, she smiled at her guards. No point in wasting the opportunity. *You want to see me naked. You want to use me one last time.*

Commanding them to do what they had planned anyway was no effort. A little involuntary blood donation by each of them didn't exhaust her powers either, just the opposite. Thus entertained and fed, she felt ready for the next step.

You will unlock the cuffs. You will provide me with an evac suit.

10

You will put me in the airlock, take my uniform, and leave. You will only remember fucking me and spacing me — naked and cuffed.

The ship's computer would record a full emergency airlock cycle — opening and closing the inner door, opening the outer door without first evacuating the lock, closing it again. The sudden decompression would have stunned any unprepared person inside, and the rush of air would have swept her out — with the ship still running at a significant part of light speed, no protective suit would have shielded her against interstellar particles.

Syreen was prepared. The evac suit protected her against the effects of decompression, and by holding to a handrail, she wasn't swept away. When the outer door closed and the lock filled with air again, she sat down and listened.

She sensed no one in the near vicinity, so she'd remain undisturbed.

Time for SitOps.

Situation — I'm alone in hostile territory and seemingly unarmed. No, that's not true, if mental weapons count. As long as I remain unseen, I'm safe, but I need provisions. I will have to move before this ship reaches its destination. In the end, I'll have to leave this ship, preferably without leaving traces.

Options — I can stay in this lock for another while, perhaps until after the next jump. I can move out at any time. I must avoid internal surveillance and recorded operations — sadly, that includes opening this lock.

Once I'm inside the ship, I can feed. I can make people forget. And I can make sure that at least this battle cruiser will never reach Brannock.

So, what can I do about this door?

A few cycles later, she had to admit to herself that, while able to open the door any time, she couldn't do anything to stop this event being recorded and reported.

I should have stayed inside the ship. Hiding here seemed like a

11

smart move, but it wasn't. Now I need a smarter move.

Perhaps she simply had to wait until someone used the airlock anyway.

Or until someone comes close enough. Until then, I can wait.

Meanwhile, she listened to the nearest stars' melancholic and soothing melodies. They didn't care about mankind's moots and moods. They just were, they just sang.

Mass and matter, gravity and germination, planets pampered with heat and light, comets caught and rarely released — for her, those were melodies of eternal beauty.

The harsh five-sigma jump came like a cold shower, even though she had sensed the ship's emitters reaching out.

A new star sang a new song, telling of multiple planets. Tiny objects defied its gravity, moved along freely, pierced the planes recklessly — hurting their harmony.

The *Oppression* should slow down now, unfold her sails, recharge — instead Syreen felt the large ship accelerate.

What are they up to?

CHAPTER SIX

The battle cruiser slowed down again and changed its course. With the central star as the nearest beacon, Syreen could easily follow its movements even without navigation panels and screens. They were clearly pulling up alongside another vessel—a much larger one, so that had to be a merchant.

Why would Admiral Tas move his battle cruiser around to inspect a merchant—a task his frigates were perfectly suited for? Did his crew need the extra drill, or were there too many merchants to be inspected? Such inspections weren't part of his mission orders, after all.

There could only be one reason, and it should mean trouble for that merchant . . . and his ship's cat, if he had taken one along.

She'd interfere with that.

Soon she sensed a group of men approaching. There was a mixture of curiosity, hunger, lust, and poorly restrained violence.

How can they maintain discipline while allowing this kind of misdemeanor? No — it must be a kind of vent. Discipline aboard, anarchy outside. This time, you'll find a different flavor of anarchy though.

Syreen moved to the side of the lock and waited. When the six men of the inspection party entered, she instructed them, *Ignore me.*

By following the six soldiers out of the airlock, Syreen soon

13

reached the merchant ship's bridge, where its crew had already assembled. All except one, she noted. As clearly as she could sense concern in the merchants, she could feel the fear of another person in the adjacent mess.

The inspection party leader didn't even try to cover their true intentions. He simply asked, "Where is she?"

The merchant captain pointed to the door. "Mess."

When the whole party left, Syreen followed. As ordered, merchants and soldiers ignored her.

One by one, the six men entered the mess. Syreen had to order the last one to step aside so she could get inside, too.

A girl in skimpy shorts and top squeezed into a corner, looking down at the floor and trembling.

No! She's not even grown up!

Syreen had to fight her own anger. Killing these men while still aboard the merchant would do no good. They had to return to the *Oppression,* and she'd return with them. Firstly, because changing ship while still deep inside AP territory wasn't safe, and secondly, because she couldn't let them get away with actions like this. For Duchy Fleet crew, abuse of civilians—including rape—under the pretense of military protocol counted as rogue action, and was treated like piracy. For AP crew, the official regulation—as stated in *AP Raydancer's* library—regarded this kind of behavior toward *irregular passengers* mainly as misconduct. That was another topic making Syreen feel sick, now that she thought about it.

Freeze. Don't move.

The first two men had only just opened their suits, had been about to pull them down. Stooping over, they now offered their necks at a convenient height for her bite.

She only took a fraction of their blood—enough to make them feel weak, to make herself feel strong.

You had your go. Next two.

Their blood tasted of lust and hate. It was a bitter taste, not the full sweetness of passion she knew, but its nutritional value was okay all the same. She felt her powers grow.

Syreen didn't need the extra power the blood of the last two would give her, but she bit them anyway.

You've got what you came for. You will leave now.

The men filed away.

Their designated victim finally dared to look up, probably wondering why her rape hadn't begun yet.

Syreen smiled at her. "You're spared today."

"Who are you?"

"You have no need to know. You won't tell anybody anyway."

The girl shook her head vigorously. "No, of course not. Are you some kind of angel?"

"You could say so."

"May I thank you?"

"Sure."

The next moment, the girl wrapped her arms around Syreen's neck and kissed her. Surprised, Syreen let it happen, and soon she felt a tongue between her lips.

Under different circumstances, she'd have answered this hunger for passion in kind, but she had to return to *Oppression* together with the inspection team. So she gave the girl a gentle mental nudge and unwrapped herself from the hug, then smiled and walked out.

She met the inspection team at the airlock, swapped ships with them, and then followed them to their quarters.

In a quiet corner, she waited for the next jump.

CHAPTER SEVEN

The jump was smooth. Obviously Torres had understood her lessons, and she appreciated that professionally.

For a while, she listened to the nearest star's song. She learned that it had no planets, so the small fleet would probably only pause here to recharge. That would give her sufficient time to deal with the members of the recent inspection team.

Ordinary crew members shared twin cabins and usually worked on different shifts, so that each had at least temporary privacy. Privacy was also the objective for resticting surveillance in crew areas.

When one of her targets returned to his cabin, she followed him, waited until he had opened his door — and then she sank her fangs into his neck.

Within a centicycle, she sucked him dry.

The beast in her rejoiced. *Oh, that sweet rush of power!*

Once Syreen regained her balance, she pushed his emptied body onto the cabin floor, where his cabin mate would later find him, stepped aside, and let the door close.

She already sensed the next two crew members approaching, considered whether to take them right away, and opted against it. She had to be unpredictable. Leaving a clear trail wouldn't be smart. Where were the other inspection team members? One radiated anger and pain—he seemed to be fighting, most likely in the ship gym.

She smiled. Anger and pain would add spice to his taste.

Now you will learn true horror.

Her two designated next victims were wrestling. She watched their fight with fascination—both men were naked, brawny, sweating, and panting, and trying to get a firm hold of the opponent while avoiding being held.

It looks like the complicated dance of two comets in a multi-star system.

Her gaze followed one of the two comets, came to a rest between his legs, on a quite impressive tool dangling back and forth. It reminded her of *Assiduous*, of her last full integration.

I'm missing my ship.

Syreen allowed herself to fantasize about herself and the wrestler's tool—what would it look like full-grown, and how would it feel inside her?

How would that blood-filled member feel inside her *mouth?* And how would it feel to suck it dry? To drain her victim through his most precious part?

Gory. Very gory – and while I can command everyone to ignore me, I can't command the blood stains to vanish. I don't need soaked gear now, thanks.

Keeping her beast at bay with comfort considerations, how awkward was that?

Most of all, I'm not here for my own fun. I'm still Duchy officer, as far as I know still Fleet Commander in Charge, so I'm still bound to Duchy Rules Of Engagement. Even if I can determine the ROE level, even if our enemy doesn't care about rules at all, I'm bound to commonly accepted limits of warfare.

Biting enemies isn't covered by any regulations. It's not limited either, though, and using the enemy's resources to regain strength is acceptable by common standards.

Finally, what these bullies had planned for that merchant's girl is mentioned in those common standards, and it's called piracy. The inspection team is guilty, and so their commanding officers are guilty, too. Which makes this vessel a pirate ship. According to standing Duchy rules, it must be destroyed.

Again, Syreen gazed at her victims. They were still watching each other, still prepared for a defensive move, but neither of them was about to launch an attack. Instead, they had both grown considerable boners.

Tempting? While she wouldn't deny herself the pleasure of mounting such a tool, those men hadn't deserved to touch her.

Not here, not today, not AP staff. Let's keep it pro.

On the other hand, how often will I find my designated prey in such a favorable situation? Stark naked, wet, and hard? I can at least watch them come.

She focused on one. *Help yourself.*

CHAPTER EIGHT

Freeze and watch.

Both men looked up in surprise. No longer commanded to ignore the Navigator, they now faced a pretty young woman, assumedly a crewmate. They were terribly aware of their own nudity, and worse, of holding their still erect cocks, from where the last remainders of their loads dripped down on the floor.

They weren't allowed to cover and hide their privates, nor were they able to turn away or to utter some weak excuse.

Both could only wait for her approach, and when she sank her fangs into the first man's neck, the other had to watch in horror.

Again, the rush of power almost overwhelmed her, but she held on. At first, she had to take the blood as fast as it came, but soon the flow ebbed away together with the man's dwindling life. She let him down, observed the bite marks close, and turned.

The second man's eyes said *No.*

Syreen could sense his terror, and her beast could sense it, too. *No,* she echoed. *I'm the master. Whether it's a savage predator on some backwater planet or my own voracity, I remain in control.*

Her fangs found his carotid, she smelled his blood, sensed his pain — her beast fought for freedom, she fought back — *I'm in control* — she soothed her victim's pain, made him relax, made him dream away from the terror, and thus pacified her beast, too.

I'm in control.

19

When she had drained him, she placed him next to the other and left.

At the door, she glanced back at the two men, sprawled across their own load, pale and lifeless, one face twisted in horror, the other's features dreamily relaxed.

I'm in control. Next one.

She met number four waiting at a junction of the central corridor. If she interpreted his feelings correctly, he was about to intercept a female crewmate on the way to her cabin, and there'd be some blackmail involved.

Syreen wasn't surprised. The lack of discipline aboard *APS Oppression* was evident. Although the Association was desperately hiring female staff for its growing fleet, their leaders obviously weren't willing to change their chauvinistic, male-centered ways.

Not that it's much different elsewhere, even in the Duchy. But who am I to complain? I'm the one in charge – because I'm the only one left. A hundred percent female staff, beat that. Haha.

She approached her victim from behind. "Hi there."

He turned and stared at her. "Oh – uh – hi."

Syreen smiled and thus bared her fangs.

His eyes widened, his legs trembled. His emotions told of horror. Running was not an option available to him, though – his fate was already sealed.

There was a mental shriek of panic when she sank her teeth into his cervical artery. When she commanded him to relax, it wasn't for mercy but for her own comfort. Panic made his blood taste bad.

At this point, she wasn't desperate for more power, even though her beast tried to suggest it to her. She didn't need his blood. It was just a question of executing her sentence – he had to be sucked dry, and there was nobody but her to suck him. Of course, like any spaceship captain, she wouldn't deny any extra power as long as she could hold it, and she could.

So, once she had finished him off, she turned toward number five.

CHAPTER NINE

Seven crew members had died in a mysterious way, and *Oppression's* entire staff was on the verge of panic. There were no traces, no recordings, no explanations — only that the seven males had been drained of almost all of their blood.

Rumor had it that the spirits of past crimes had manifested in soul sucking ghouls, haunting evildoers for their sins. Syreen didn't feel like a ghoul, but wouldn't disagree with the reasoning.

People were warily looking over their shoulders while walking down corridors in groups of four or more. When they reached their cabins, when they had to part, their fear became almost tangible.

Syreen wasn't surprised when command announced it would skip recharging after the next jump. Again they had reached a lone star, another pivot system, not worth a second look for ordinary humans who couldn't appreciate its eternal song.

Two guards were now protecting each officer, operating in shifts, changing every two cycles.

When the relief entered Admiral Tas' quarters, she followed them inside. *Ignore me* was their standing order. This wouldn't do for the admiral, though.

She stepped before his desk.

Watch me.

He looked up. "If you dare to enter here without appointment, you'd better salute appropriately."

Amused, she stood to attention and produced a salute that

would have made her drill sergeant proud. "Fleet Commander in Charge Syreen, Duchy Fleet, reporting, *Sir!*"

"Duchy Fleet? What's that nonsense?"

"No nonsense, Admiral. AP fleet attacked the Duchy without advance declaration of war. As the only surviving officer, it is my duty to exercise counterstrikes as I deem necessary. Moreover, like every Duchy officer, it is my duty to leave no act of piracy unpunished. According to our regulations, this includes abuse or rape of civil staff aboard merchant ships like the one your crew inspected two stops ago."

The elder officer shook his head. "Girl, I don't know what game you're playing, but I'm in no mood for such mockery. You'd better return to your quarters and wait for disciplinary action. Who's your superior?"

"The Duke only, Sir, and only if he's free and able to make his decisions alone. Which, I fear, currently is not the case."

He opened his eyes and for the first time seemed to recognize her as one not of his crew. "You're serious. You must be insane to visit me aboard my own ship, within my quarters, guarded by my crew, and threaten me."

"You are not safe here, aboard your own ship, within your quarters, guarded by no one."

"So, what are your plans then? You try to kill me and escape?"

"No, Admiral Tas. No tries. I *will* kill you, and after the next jump, I will destroy your ship. Only then will I escape."

"Enough of this nonsense. Guards, arrest her."

Nothing happened.

Syreen waited.

Eventually, he swallowed. "What's going on here?"

"Admiral, I don't owe you explanations, and you won't live long enough to profit from them anyway. Let's just say you — the AP — took a bite too large to swallow."

When she stepped around his desk and unveiled her fangs,

23

and his guards still didn't move, he realized the truth in her statement.

Chapter Ten

The admiral wasn't missed until after the next jump. With the next shift of guards' arrival, Syreen left his office, leaving two guards in dire need of explanations behind.

On her way to the engines, she cautiously avoided the ship's eyes—if necessary, she hid her face from the cameras behind and between groups of crew members, and her evac suit was inconspicuous enough for the computer.

Oppression's engines hummed with deceleration while the ship descended deeper into the system. The local star sang of planets. Not Brannock yet, but a system where she could find a different ship.

Flag Captain Munoz was kind enough to bring her close to the harbor. She'd make him sail even closer. A little power plant failure would surely convince him to extend his stay and enjoy the local hospitality.

When the engineer on duty turned to sign the pad of a junior noncom, she suggested a minor change of protocol to the operator. The aft emitter ducts needed more heating, and its emitters should run a thorough test cycle.

Each procedure was harmless in itself. Each of the ship's ducts, passages and compartments could be heated or cooled in reaction to or preparation for events the computer couldn't see or foresee. So it wasn't unusual to override the automatic climate control and heat up the ducts.

Emitter test cycles were standard business, too. Every now and then, individual emitters or groups of them could be subjected to thorough tests, either because they had already

25

shown signs of wear, or in preparation for critical actions when they shouldn't fail. To this end, the tests had to put emitters under substantial stress.

The stress test would cause the emitters to heat up. Usually, the ducts would automatically be cooled accordingly. However, as the computer had been told to heat them up — in preparation for a frosty event that would never come — this time, the overheating would make most of the casings break.

Syreen remembered well what a broken casing looked like, and she also remembered well how such a damage had almost cost her life.

No skipper with a sane mind would attempt a jump with emitters with broken casing. However, how would he know? The tests weren't meant to show broken casings, but broken emitters, and the emitters weren't broken yet. Just the opposite — the unplanned test would show perfectly working machinery.

However, once the ship entered hyperspace, the emitters would blow up, the protective sphere would pop, and the ship and its crew would disappear without a trace.

This is war.

Next, she had to mess with the power plant.

CHAPTER ELEVEN

Flag Captain Munoz tested Syreen's patience. He stayed in orbit above Wagaki for five full tencycles. His engineers were probably happy about the extra time to fix, check and recheck their primary power plant, while Syreen tried to avoid attracting more attention.

The ship was subject to searches several times, none of which uncovered the admiral's killer. Instead, the investigations unveiled illegal drugs, misappropriated equipment, and some quite unusual sex toys. Now and then, crew members reported to sick bay, claiming to feel weak, but the medical analysis didn't produce any reasons except for low blood readings—the ship doctor began to wonder whether anemia could be contagious.

The people were on edge, which made their minds difficult to control. Syreen had to focus on each individual to make him or her look away and ignore her. These efforts drained her powers quicker than she had expected, and the beast demanded to be fed more frequently.

Syreen recognized a downward spiral when she saw one, and she knew that she had to leave soon.

When the ship's doctor requested additional provisions, to be procured at Wagaki Orbital, she grabbed the opportunity and a new uniform and joined him on the shuttle.

Getting in was hard. Syreen had to shift her attention between the doctor and his two assistants, the two guards at the hangar door, and the pilot, and couldn't afford letting any of them go for more than a few blinks.

Once she had assumed her seat in the last row, she could ease her efforts. As long as nobody turned around, she was fine.

For a few centicycles, she could relax and listen to Wagaki's song. Here, as in many of the younger systems, the main planet and the central star shared the same name. It seemed appropriate to her, although the original settlers couldn't have known that the central star's song echoed through its planets, and more so for systems with only one planet, like Wagaki.

There was so much beauty in these songs — a pity that humans couldn't hear them.

All too soon, the shuttle arrived and docked at the orbital station. Now Syreen had to focus on its passengers again. *Just don't look back.*

She was the last to leave the shuttle. In port, she allowed the locals to notice her presence, so that camera imagery and human memories would match, at least in numbers. At the first opportunity, she took a side corridor.

Only after two more turns, alone in another narrow passage, did she allow herself to relax.

Time for SitOps. Wagaki is AP territory and thus still a hostile environment. My arrival has been recorded. Correction — the arrival of a nameless female AP captain has been recorded. At some point, her image will be matched against a Captain Ishtar Gryf, and against a certain escapee from Nysa. Once that word arrives here, I'm busted.

This AP uniform is no longer useful. I should change identity soon.

Ways to leave. I could try to steal a ship. Hard to achieve, if at all.

I could sign up on a merchant vessel as their new navigator. What would I do with their old one? Moreover, that'd be like putting up a Shoot me *sign.*

I could play ship's cat again. Perhaps even sneak on the ship un-recorded? I needn't be picky — once we're on our way, I can make the crew ignore me. No need to play the star angel card.

She smiled. *That's a plan.*

A young man smiled back, having appeared from nowhere and now obviously feeling encouraged to approach her. With his tousled hair, the clean lavender jumpsuit, and the soft shoes, she'd have gladly welcomed him to her bed — another day, another place. Here and now, he was an additional witness she couldn't afford. She shouldn't have let her guard down.

Syreen's gaze fell on the clean-shaven skin over his carotid. She almost heard his pounding heart, felt the blood rushing through his arteries and veins, tasted iron on her tongue.

The lavender man paused. His puzzled look answered the sudden expression of hunger in her face.

No. Not here, not now.

She had to make an effort to keep her beast at bay before she could reassure her designated victim. Another smile, this time deliberately lecherous, should do the trick.

"Your place or mine?"

That question caught him on the wrong foot. "Uh — I — your place — aboard?"

She kicked her shoes away and unbuttoned her jacket. "Wherever I drop my shoes, that's my place. Are you ready?"

"Um — here?"

"You know a better place?"

It was so cute, watching him trying to collect his wits. Her blouse zipper coming down didn't help at all.

But finally, he succeeded. "Um — there's a maintenance staff room right up this hallway. It should be empty at this time."

CHAPTER TWELVE

Syreen smelled the people before she heard the music — and the music was almost deafening. A thought brushed the wave of excitement attacking her mental barriers away.

A pity I can't repel that olfactory attack as easily.

With her newly procured — well, stolen — shirt and pants she felt prepared enough to meet strangers, but that music bar was no place to negotiate . . . verbally. She'd have to resort to other means of communication.

In this part of the station, the light bluish coloring of walls and floor had disappeared under a convergent layer of gray and brown smears. The soles of her shoes seemed to stick and probably wouldn't even lose their grip in zero G. No, she wouldn't try to find out about the walls.

How could anyone feel comfortable in such a mess? And how could the station command let it run down that far? The Duchy wouldn't have allowed this kind of negligence.

She sighed. *I don't know anything about my former home, how the people fare, what the Association is doing to them. I should find out.*

No. She paused. *I should find out what to do about it. That's what I came for, and that's still my mission, even though I'm currently exercising a tactical retreat.*

Syreen turned around a corner. The actual sight of the bar entrance made it even worse, not just for the flock of dirty people hanging around, but also for the liquids spilled all over the floor, forming a small lake — was it just forwine and beer, or what else could be mixed up with it? She'd better not

30

ask.

To her, the dirty look of place and people meant something else — merchants feeling attracted might be interested in picking up a ship's cat, and might be willing to smuggle one aboard without letting the authorities know. That was what she needed — to get away unrecorded. Everything else would put up a sign for her pursuers.

There had to be pursuers, once they learned how she had left Nysa. If they didn't know already anyway.

A beefy guy near the door ogled her chest. When she reached the entrance, he barred her way with one arm. "No hookers here."

For a moment, she was taken aback. How should she answer his insult? Unleash her beast on him? Or swallow it and just make him stand back with her mental powers?

No. *Keep your cover, gal.*

Syreen smiled at him and ambled away with swaying hips. She could feel his gaze stuck to her buttocks until she turned around the next corner.

She could easily wait for her targets to leave the venue.

Syreen had heard the senior man being called "Skipper" and "Mo" and "Poppa" — he was owner and captain of the long-haul freighter *Molly Malone,* bound for Gattaca.

She hadn't heard of Gattaca before, and from what she learned by listening to his crew, she'd rather have remained innocent. Gattaca was a quarantine planet, and the inhabitants were the offspring of illegal genetic experiments.

Let evolution sort out that mess, was the only official statement, according to Poppa. Wait until Gattaca's *hospitable biology* has eradicated past atrocities.

Until then, the orbital research station needed its annual provisioning, and *Molly Malone* was supposed to deliver it.

Syreen wasn't interested in Gattaca — just the opposite, it

probably was the last place she'd want to stay, even worse than Appalahoo.

No. Actually, the last place she'd want to be was on the same ship with that filthy bunch of men. When she began suggesting that they take her along unregistered, she met no resistance. Just the opposite — and there was something on their minds that almost frightened her.

Not that she had much choice if she wanted to depart soon. So she followed them through narrow maintenance passages and doors that should have been locked, until Poppa stopped next to an airlock. Symbols for radioactive, acidic and electric hazards didn't make it look promising.

Explain, she commanded.

"The regular airlock is right above us," Poppa said. "This one provides access to the plumbing. Water feed, waste drain, reactor mass. But it's also a way to get certain . . . goods onto the ship unrecorded. Obviously, we shouldn't be here, and we won't enter here — the crew's return to the ship must be recorded. But for you, it's safe."

Safe enough, his expression gave away.

She shrugged. "Okay."

"We will need a quartercycle to get aboard. Haiki will open the ship lock for you. You shouldn't enter too early, but don't be late either. Haiki can't keep that lock open forever."

The shaggy engineer nodded. His mental aura wasn't overly inviting, either, but Syreen was sure she could handle him.

"See you aboard." The merchant captain left, and his crew followed.

CHAPTER THIRTEEN

I'm a monster, Syreen mused. *Drinking my victims' blood, pulling their strings, making them dance to my tune.*

Almost a quartercycle had passed since they had left. She opened the airlock and entered the small chamber.

When the station-side door closed, she held her breath. But the lights signaled *all clear,* and the outer door slid away. A cold rush of air made her shiver — of course. The maintenance duct wasn't heated. The little warmth she'd need to survive came from the tubes' imperfect insulation, and perhaps from the station air rushing in during previous crossings.

They didn't bother to tell me about warmer clothing. Or about protection against cosmic radiation. Bastards.

She moved through the narrow duct as fast as she could. No need to expose herself longer than necessary.

Open the ship airlock.

Surely Haiki would have let her wait, just for the fun of it. She could sense his malice. However, he had no choice but to do her bidding. The door slid away the very moment she arrived, and closed right behind her.

He stared at her and licked his lips. She didn't have to read his mind to recognize his intentions, and moved closer. First of all, his body was a welcome source of warmth. Second, his little blood donation was just a little extra to replenish the power she'd had to spend on mind control.

Haiki would remember nothing but the quickie she'd suggested.

"Now?" she asked.

33

"I'll check the livestock. Come along?"

Again, there was a glimpse of malice in his mind. What was he up to now?

Whatever it might be, she felt able to handle it. "Go ahead."

He showed her a thin smile.

Syreen followed Haiki down toward the freight section. The access reminded her of her trip with *Mary Of Skye,* of the passenger with the head injury they had taken along. *How does that unknown miner fare today?*

Her guide opened a door and pointed inside. "Have a look."

She recognized twelve container beds with hibernation equipment. Each of it held the peaceful face of a sleeping beauty.

What the abyss?

"Explain."

Even without a mental nudge, Haiki shrank back. "Entertainers for Gattaca. The researchers are very lonely there. They need some company now and then."

"Why in hibernation?"

"It's cheaper this way."

She slowly shook her head. "Not true. Their beds take up more space than a passenger bunk would, and consume extra power. They need expensive nutrients . . ." What was that look on his face? "What do you feed them?"

"A sugar solution. It will keep them alive, as always."

"You mean, you do that regularly?" There was still something terribly wrong here. "What happens with the women you carried last time? You take them back?"

Haiki didn't have to answer.

"No, you don't. So, what about them? Tell me." *Tell me.*

"When we get there, they are gone. I don't know—"

Tell me.

"One time, one of the techies bragged about a *farewell party.*

34

They banged the remaining girls in groups, and then—well, they sent them dirtside with camera drones and watched the wildlife hunting them down."

Syreen swallowed—and it took all her self-control not to kill the man right there and then.

"Well." She pointed at the containers. "Take good care of them. I would feel very displeased should anything happen to them."

The engineer flinched. He obviously couldn't match her icy command voice with the ship's cat she was supposed to be.

"But . . ."

"I'll find the way to the bridge myself, thank you."

Merchants are very much built alike. There's no budget for extravagance. Freight, aggregates, maintenance ducts, and the crew squeezed into space not otherwise usable. Including the bridge.

Guidance by the other crew members' mental emanations wasn't necessary, although it reassured Syreen. They had all gathered on the bridge, exchanging inspiring, if not arousing, ideas Syreen didn't have to listen to in order to find out that she was the subject of their fantasies.

When she appeared in the doorway and all gazes fell on her stern face, she felt their fantasies shatter like broken glass.

"We will depart now."

"You've got no say—" the captain protested.

"We're scheduled to depart. You will do what is needed."

The pilot suddenly drew a knife and moved toward her.

Freeze, all.

"Yusef, right?"

Drop that knife.

The blade dropped from Yusef's powerless fingers.

Syreen walked across to him and caressed his neck with a finger. "Be nice, boy. We'll have our fun later."

Yusef couldn't match her icy voice with her lascivious words and gesture, but she could sense his mind adjusting to her presence and unspoken requests. He would cause no trouble.

"Okay, guys." She clapped her hands. "You've got work to do. You wouldn't want to trigger the attention of the guys in that AP battle cruiser out there, would you? You wouldn't want to be subject of a thorough inspection, which surely would raise the issue of your livestock cargo. So, go ahead and ignore my presence for now."

Keep calm and stand back, gal. She retreated to the aft bulkhead and watched them preparing *Molly Malone* for departure.

I'm no longer sure who's the monster here — me and my beast, or those bastards with their gruesome cargo. But I can't do anything about them while we're still in the same system with APS Oppression *and its flotilla, or in the same system with any AP warship, anyway. Okay, I could seize their minds and make them do anything — it's okay while it's about their dealing with me, but it's not okay about their ship. Taking their ship, by whatever means, would be piracy. I'm still Duchy Fleet Commander in Charge. I can borrow an enemy warship, but I can't hijack a merchant. I just can't.*

Which brings up the question what I can *do. Leave those poor women to their fate? If it was about sex, even rape, I might shrug and turn away, but they'll be used as live prey for entertainment!*

Stop.

Again, she had to fight her growing rage.

Stop. Anger is a bad advisor. I'm a Navigator, I'm better than that.

Syreen focused inward — without letting her mental control drop — and listened to the central star's song again.

I still need a plan. Getting away from here isn't enough. Not any longer.

CHAPTER FOURTEEN

Molly Malone slowly accelerated toward her designated jump point. While Syreen watched, the men checked their displays several times — primarily plot and radio.

Their main concern was *APS Oppression* with her four escorts. The small flotilla had left the vicinity of Wagaki Orbital a few cycles later, was heading roughly toward the same jump point, and was therefore closing the distance to the merchant. So far, they hadn't announced any intention to meet, but what if they'd make up their minds to carry out an inspection?

Syreen wasn't worried, only curious. Flag Captain Munoz had his mission orders, and he was already late. His *master* wouldn't accept an unplanned and unnecessary merchant ship inspection as excuse for further delay, that much she could guess.

"Skipper?"

"What's up, Yusef?"

"A new arrival. Navy entry point, little shock. What's so special about Wagaki that they're now shaking hands here?"

"Your guess is as good as mine. How many, what type?"

They had to wait until *Molly Malone's* sensors picked up the transponder code.

"Only a corvette."

The captain took a deep breath, and then smiled. "Well, a corvette won't cause us trouble. Unless it's that Brannock jockey, eh?"

"Unlikely, Mo."

No, that Brannock jockey's watching your back, guys, only you don't know it.

"How long?" the captain asked.

"Another quartercycle. That school will jump sooner, I reckon. Oops—they're gone." Yusef leaned over his board. "What's that? There's a strange jitter in that hypershock—I don't think the big ship did a smooth jump."

"Show me."

The captain examined Yusef's data. After a moment, he whistled.

"Yusef, do you remember what I told you about broken emitters, and why you shouldn't risk a jump with those? I've seen example measures of jumps with minor damage. This is how a truly big fuck-up would look. Poor souls."

"But how can that happen? In the navy?"

"That's the question, ain't it? I know there's some slack in the AP navy sometimes, but they usually keep their vital stuff tidy."

"But not this time."

"No."

They frowned at each other.

Syreen could feel Mo considering cancellation of their jump. She couldn't allow that to happen, so she stepped forward. "Someone must have messed with their emitter lines."

Rather unwillingly, the captain turned to her. His expression said—how could a ship's cat speak up on such a topic? "What do you know about emitters?"

"You need them for jumps, that's all I need to know. And if they should be okay, but weren't, it's sabotage. Which means they must have pissed someone off. Mightily."

"But that someone would die with them."

"Not if that someone left them at Wagaki."

Understanding dawned in the skipper's expression. "What could possibly piss someone off so mightily as to sabotage a ship's hyperjump emitters?"

"For example, shooting down a mostly civil orbital station

without advance declaration of war?"

He stared at her. "That would be outrageous! I mean, we're no choir boys by any means, but . . ."

The skipper's voice trailed off. He buried his face in his hands. "Who would do that?"

"The AP navy did."

"When, where?"

"Some kilocycles ago, in the Duchy."

"The Duchy. Where's that?"

Yusef stepped in. "Near Kyris. You remember that story about the *Light of Mandalay's* rescue, Poppa?"

"The pirate killer?"

"Rumor has it, 'twas a Duchy pilot."

"Crap." The captain turned to Syreen again. "And how would a mere ship's cat have learned about all that?"

Yusef eyed her curiously.

His captain waved a hand. "Because this ship's cat isn't what she pretends to be. Am I right, gal?"

Syreen sighed inwardly. Again she had blown her cover. She could make them forget, but should she? She shrugged.

"You're right. And to answer your next questions, I'm the one who messed with their emitters. I'm also the Brannock jockey and the pirate killer. I'm a pilot in the Duchy Fleet, therefore I'm at war with the AP."

"Operating independently? Where did you get your orders?"

"I don't get orders, Captain. I'm all that's left of Fleet, so I'm Fleet Commander in Charge."

"Fleet Commander, huh? I should say you're pulling my leg, but somehow I tend to believe you—there's at least one sure thing, that AP battle cruiser couldn't survive its jump. Your biggest kill?"

"No. I've sabotaged a dreadnaught before."

His eyes narrowed. "You're not one I'd like to have on my

bad side."

She returned his glare. "Do you have a good side I could get on?"

Now he shrugged. "As I said, we're no choir boys. We're trying to run with the wolves, you know? Do as you're told, don't be picky with your contracts, don't draw attention, get the job done."

"Shipping sex slaves—or should I say, live bait?"

He didn't even try to appear guilty. "Yes. I could mention our contract—we're supposed to ship the old girls out. Only there are never any left. The eggheads tell us they've chosen to go dirtside. Who are we to know better? There are rumors, nothing tangible."

"You could ask around."

"Yeah, and I could run *Molly* into a star. Security guards on Gattaca are no jolly fellows. When you see one, you don't ask questions, and you can see one wherever you go."

"You could stop shipping new slaves."

"Yes, and then someone else will get the contract. I know, I know, that's lame. If no one takes the contract, this business will dry out. But do you think no one would do it?" He didn't wait for her reply. "So we're the ones doing the dirty work. What else could we do about it?"

"End it."

"That's easily said."

"I know it's not easy. I'm not taking the easy way out."

"No." His gaze dropped to her chest. "No, you don't. Playing the ship's cat to get a passage—isn't that humiliating?"

"It is. But that doesn't matter. The greatest humiliation is that I can't help my fellow countrymen yet. In comparison, my dignity and physical discomfort count for nothing. My body is but a tool in war, utilized in any way that helps my cause."

"So. And what should we do with you now?"

"Take me to Gattaca."

"Where you . . ."

She winked. "Let's do one jump at a time. We're about due, aren't we?"

"We are," the captain agreed.

That was the moment the pilot spoke up. "Skipper? Incoming call from Wagaki."

"Now? Hold it, Yusef. What could they want?"

"Probably asking us to return," Syreen said. "But if you jump *right now,* you can say you missed it."

He frowned, but only for a blink. "Right. Jump."

Yusef acknowledged with a nod.

Molly Malone jumped.

Chapter Fifteen

Syreen struggled to get back on her knees. When she looked around, she saw the others not faring much better—only they were buckled to their seats.

The captain grinned at her. "Sorry. But you were right—there was no time left to offer you a seat."

She grinned back. "I've felt worse. You jump at four-sigma?"

"Let's say, we're taking a special route. That way we're less likely to encounter pirates."

"No need to strain your ship and crew. You could have done the same jump with five-sigma."

"You haven't even seen our data and think you can already run us down?"

"Sorry if it sounded that way." She rose to her feet. "I could feel it—there was room for improvement, and one or two sigma levels each jump will save you a lot of money."

He calmed down quickly, and she smirked.

Nothing soothes a merchant as much as caring about his money.

For this jump, it was good as it was. A six-sigma hyper-shock would have given her away like putting up a sign.

"You can *feel* it?"

"I will offer you a calculation for the next jump. Then it's your call."

The captain glanced at his pilot. "Well, it can't do much harm to have a look."

So far, it had all been a friendly chitchat. The skipper had bought her story quite quickly, or so it had appeared. Now Syreen had to deliver on it.

Yusef had prepared his solution and then offered her his blank console.

She smiled and called up the star map.

Their next stop should be Hawthorne. There was an official route from Wagaki to Hawthorne via Robbins—she hadn't heard either name before—with one unnamed pivotal system on each leg, but *Molly Malone's* first jump had led them on a different path. That much she knew, and now the ship computer provided her with their current position.

She recognized the idea. Four more easy-to-calculate five-sigma jumps would take them to Hawthorne without visiting another inhabited system. It was a smart choice of route, and she nodded at Yusef.

With a little more effort, she could optimize two of these jumps to six-sigma. Seven would be possible, but only if she taught *Molly Malone* the necessary formulas, and she wouldn't give that knowledge away now.

She finalized that calculation and started a new one. Her fingers rushed across the board, picked new nodes, triggered computer proposals, refined parameters, and added her solution to the first.

"Done." She transferred both her solutions to the captain's desk.

"Already?" he asked. "Quick and dirty, eh? Navy approach?"

"Navy approach." Syreen nodded and smiled.

Mo started to examine her results. "Hey—you've planned the whole route? Not just one jump? What . . . bugger me. Six-sigma, and another one!" He looked up. "That's excellent. Yusef, check that. That gal knows her business indeed."

"Check my other solution," Syreen said.

"Another? Heck, you had no time—by all-star demons,

what's that? Only three jumps, and all six-sigma?"

He stared at her. "Gal, if you're not the best navigator I've ever heard of . . ."

She shrugged and smiled. "Navy approach."

The captain nodded. "Yes, and I see a pattern here. Precision. That's how you did it, right? How you shot them?"

Yusef was still examining her solutions. "Unbelievable," he muttered and shook his head. "So fast."

"Precision is key," Syreen agreed.

"You surely were teaching navigation in your Fleet, right?" the captain dug deeper.

"Skirmisher pilot."

"What's that?"

"Basically seat, gun and engine wrapped in steel. Very agile."

"Like a stingship then."

"Smaller."

"But jump-capable?"

"No."

"But . . ." His voice trailed off. Next, he shook his head. "No matter. Yusef, which of the three solutions would you prefer?"

"I? Mo, if I had to do it, I'd take the second—her first—because that's a route I can handle. I see what she did there, and it's outstanding. Still, her second route is so much better—but it's beyond me. However, as long as she's aboard, let's do it her way. Three jumps. I want to see it happen."

"I thought so. Okay, make it happen."

CHAPTER SIXTEEN

Syreen glanced at Mo, and the captain smiled back. He could really be the nice guy—since she'd blown her cover, she hadn't had resorted to her mind control at all.

The captain leaned forward in his chair. "The next jump will take us to Hawthorne—I have no doubt it will be as smooth as the last two. Navy approach?"

She nodded. "Navy approach. Or let's rather say, Duchy Fleet approach."

"Where one skirmisher pilot takes out a dreadnaught." Mo grinned. "I remember."

"You'd better not mention that on Hawthorne."

"Why?"

"The AP navy isn't particularly fond of me. They might subject you to a rather unpleasant interrogation."

"There's a price on your head?"

She glared at him.

He flinched. "Hey, just asking."

"They wouldn't leave you time to spend your pieces of silver. They'd keep you, just in case."

"Okay, okay, got the message. What if they spot you anyway?"

"There'll be blood."

The following silence gave her time to relax and listen.

Mo felt visibly uncomfortable. While he didn't hesitate to deliver young women to their doom, her mention of open violence unsettled him.

Yusef and Haiki focused on their boards and pretended to

45

be busy. Neither of them was eager to join the conversation.

Syreen didn't miss idle talk. Instead, she tuned in to the unnamed star's lament.

The more often Syreen listened, the better she could imagine some kind of meaning behind the melodies. This star seemed to sing of lonesomeness, of a loss long ago. Of being forgotten—yes, she could sympathize with that.

Her fellow Duchy pilots and superiors were gone, together with all of her friends, if she ever had any, station people she'd met and fooled around with, servers, bartenders, shuttle jockeys . . .

There'd be no one left to remember her on her own home world. There'd be few Duchy citizens at all, perhaps on Kyris, and those had other worries to care about.

Some traders she'd met and traveled with might remember the navigator, but for most of them, she'd be a fading memory by now.

A few people who should remember her had been told to forget.

My crew? Stephan, Herman, Drake, Crow? Left behind on some backwater planet, busy with their own survival—would they find time to think of me? Hardly. Basically, I'm forgotten, like my People are. I'm indeed one of the Forgotten People, truthfully called so.

When *Molly Malone* established her jump field, Syreen sent out a mental goodbye. She didn't expect the star to answer, but she imagined receiving a distant sigh in return. Next, they were gone.

PART TWO—ESCAPE

CHAPTER SEVENTEEN

Mo admired his passenger's serene smile. There was as much beauty in her figure and in her attitude as in her jump calculations. It was the latter that pleased his pockets, but the former was much more comforting than he'd been willing to admit to himself initially.

He'd always told himself he was just adapting to his world — going along, trying to make a living without inviting trouble. He'd been quite successfully ignoring the ugly truth about his life.

We're not making it better, that's for sure. But we're also not just getting along. *We're abetting, we're actively making things* worse – *like for these sorry hookers we took along. We're part of the system, of a system that's broken, and instead of mending it, we're . . . well, I'm repeating myself.*

A sound interrupted his musings.

"Skipper?" Yusef repeated.

"What?" He shook his head. "Anything wrong with the jump?"

"No. We arrived at Hawthorne as planned, and old *Molly* is fine. I just thought you should know there's an AP destroyer in the system, just approaching Hawthorne Orbital."

He shrugged. "Too bad. Nothing we can do about it."

His passenger didn't seem to be overly concerned. Had she even noticed Yusef, as she wore such an absent expression?

She hadn't even told them her name — and it was probably better that way. For the records, she'd be nothing but a nameless ship's cat. But now that he wanted to address her, *Hey you* seemed inappropriate. *Well. There's always a proper way.*

"Fleet Commander?"

"Yes, Captain?"

"Yusef spotted a destroyer."

She nodded. "Yes, I heard you."

"You're not worried?"

"Why should I? AP ships are everywhere. We're just passing through."

"What if they want to inspect us?"

"No difference to Wagaki. You should worry about your livestock cargo, not about me."

Mo watched her leaving the bridge.

"Cold as a fish," Yusef commented.

"I heard that."

The door closed, and the captain smiled at his pilot. He couldn't remember ever seeing Yusef blush before.

Finally, he decided to relieve Yusef of his embarrassment. "Why don't you send our greetings to Hawthorne now and ask them whether they have a free dock for us?"

While Yusef did as instructed, Mo considered his options.

Technically, they could just make another jump. *Molly's* batteries were far from exhausted, and she had hardly started deceleration yet. It wouldn't take Yusef long to calculate a solution. Not even an AP destroyer could catch them before they were gone.

We could do it – once.

In the long run, it wouldn't do them any good. Within tencycles, they'd be on every blacklist in every port. Worse, if anyone learned why they had done it, they'd make it to the top of AP's shit list.

The same would happen if the AP inspected their ship and found their passenger – Mo had no doubts they'd recognize her, despite her disguise as ship's cat. AP records were too good to miss a known face.

One way around that was to tell them before – to sell her

out. Why didn't that option appeal to him? Because she was right—it wouldn't stop the AP asking questions? No. He could follow her reasoning, but that wasn't what bothered him.

There was something about her that touched him. Under her tough shell, she was nice and kind, someone to make friends with. More importantly, she was someone you'd want on your side when the going got tough. She had gone far out of her way to rescue a mere merchant ship when she'd been in the deepest shit herself—no AP captain would do any such thing for him.

If he could choose, he'd prefer a galaxy with more people like her and less people like those AP bullies.

But could he choose?

CHAPTER EIGHTEEN

"We're docked," Mo announced when his passenger reappeared on the bridge. "They announced an inspection team."

"I thought so. In that case, I'd better leave your ship the same way I came in, okay?" She seemed to sense his denial before he could frown. "No?"

"Sorry, no. The Hawthorne people are somewhat peculiar with regard to their harbor security—no amount of bribery could make them ease their checks. Moreover, they won't even let us connect before we're cleared."

"Okay."

She was taking the bad news well.

"I've considered an option," he said.

"Yes?"

"We could hide you among our livestock."

"You have an extra coffin?"

He made a face. He wouldn't have expected her to use such a derogatory term. "No. We can clear a bed for you."

"What about the occupant?"

"Just a ship's cat."

Mo didn't like the way her eyebrows rose.

"Inconspicuous," he quickly added. "Not on anybody's list. She'll play along, and you're safe."

"And asleep." She didn't add *at your mercy.*

"Yes. You'd have to trust me. I know that's not easy."

"Oh—I do trust you."

That statement, delivered with full sincerity, took him by

51

surprise. She was right, but how could she be so sure?

She went on, "But I don't trust the AP will ignore your cargo. Once they learn about your livestock, they'll check every face. So, thank you for your honest offer, but I must decline."

"How will you get past inspection, then?"

"I'll meet them in the mess. That's where they'd expect to find a ship's cat. We'll find out whether they recognize me or not."

The officer seemed confident she would pass that inspection, but there was another issue. "If they buy into your cover . . ."

"They'll fuck me, yes. That's much more pleasant than an AP interrogation, trust me."

Again, he could almost hear the *been there, done that* between her lines, and not relating to the former. A cold chill ran down his spine. *Poor girl.*

"If you want it that way."

"Just don't interfere."

He nodded. Sure—the last thing she'd need were additional gawkers. The *inspection* would be humiliating enough.

"I'm sorry."

She shook her head and left.

Yusef and Haiki gazed at him, but he didn't find words. So he only waved at them to proceed. Letting the inspection team wait wouldn't help them.

CHAPTER NINETEEN

Syreen sensed the inspection team's approach long before they reached *Molly Malone's* dock. Their thoughts had a special quality of malice and greed that couldn't be mistaken.

But there was a different flavor, too, a flavor she didn't know what to make of yet.

She'd deal with them as she'd dealt with inspection parties before—give them happy memories but nothing else, and take their blood in exchange. She wouldn't be mentioned in any records. Not even AP sailors were stupid enough to record a rape.

Mo had surprised her. Under his rough and business-centered shell she'd found a core of honesty. It hadn't taken much effort to touch it, and once he'd rediscovered his own virtues, he'd eagerly embraced them. If it could be so easy to bring a good man back on track, how could their galaxy have turned into this dark place?

Because nobody taught them to listen to the stars and their songs? Because nobody told them how much beauty lay in harmony and compassion?

Or because it was easier to stick to the Books instead of using one's own good judgment? Her old instructor came to her mind. Innovation and creativity weren't asked for. New ways required reports, consultations, assessments, approvals and disapprovals. New ways meant a lot of extra work for people already busy enough. If they were meant to be implemented, processes and regulations and training instructions had to be changed, too, trainers had to go back to school, already trained people needed to be re-trained, and — gasp! — even the Books might have to be rewritten in passages.

In comparison, what happened to those sailing on tested passages? They could doze in their tranquility — until a hostile fleet appeared at their airlock. Which hadn't happened in megacycles.

Regarding airlocks . . . that inspection team was about due.

Now that they were close, that different flavor tasted familiar — and made her uncomfortable. She'd sampled such taste before.

Gooey, she'd labeled it. Its source had called himself *master* and had caused her quite some discomfort.

Quite some. Who you're fooling, gal? It's been the abyss.

The current source wasn't quite as strong as that *master,* but no less despicable. She wasn't eager to meet that creature.

Not that I've got a say in it.

The inspection team visiting *Molly Malone* was unusual at seven heads strong. Four men went to the bridge, three came straight for her — or so it seemed. In any case, they entered the mess where Syreen had been waiting.

Two AP marine soldiers took position to both sides of the door. One man with lieutenant stripes on his untidy and stained, not even properly buttoned uniform slowly approached her. "See what we've got here. A pretty ho, unregistered for sure, ready for the taking."

With his messy hair, unshaved chin and cheeks, brownish stains at his teeth, she wouldn't want to let him come any closer.

Close enough. Stop.

He cocked his head, smiled, and continued his approach. "The master said you might try that. It won't work on me. I'm ordered to ignore any and all of your orders."

The master knows? How?

It probably hadn't taken him much to add two and two

together — a dead torturer, a dead officer, both drained of their blood, and no witnesses at all, and if he was able to administer mind control and she was able to withstand, she had to be one of his kin. The master knew what his kin was able to do, most likely better than she did. He only hadn't yet understood the difference between Forgotten People's males and their females, hadn't learned what a true Navigator was.

"You better surrender," her visitor said. "I'm supposed to return you alive, but I'm allowed to apply necessary violence — whatever is needed to teach you obedience. As you see, I've brought some help."

He cackled and grabbed her arm. "I don't think I need help."

No, you don't.

She turned to one side, but didn't get far. His grip was surprisingly strong.

"You won't get away that easily. Why don't you start to show some obedience? Drop your pants, and I might leave it at a few smacks on your bare ass."

Shoot him.

His eyes grew wide, his jaw dropped, showing unnaturally long canines — then the shots from two marine rifles struck his body, spraying flesh and blood over the mess' bulkhead.

That wasn't the worst.

She watched the flow of his blood stopping, his wounds shrinking, almost closing. He was healing unnaturally fast.

CHAPTER TWENTY

The healing slowed down, finally stopped before the holes in that creature's skin could entirely close.

Syreen glanced back at the two marine soldiers. They were still staring at the corpse of their fellow lieutenant, whom they had just shot down.

She sighed inwardly. Her immediate problem was solved, but this twist of events required a lot more explanations, and she couldn't come up with a good story.

Well, in that case, a bad one will do.

"He ordered you to have your guns ready, just to make a point, and that's what you did. Then he stepped forward to examine that pretty ship's cat, thus obstructing your line of fire. But you had a good sight on these boobs." She removed her shirt — showing was easier than suggesting. "You couldn't help that sudden itch in your trigger finger. You'll claim your guns had a malfunction at the worst possible moment. In any case, both the lieutenant and the ship's cat are dead. You clean up that mess, feed the organic waste to the ship's converters and leave."

She stepped out of their field of vision and watched them doing the dirty work. *You shot him, and you shot the ship's cat. Otherwise, your inspection rendered nothing unusual, nothing you wouldn't expect to find on a merchant ship provisioning an AP research station.*

They took their time cleaning up. When they were done, one of them went to the pantry and fetched a bottle. "We're in deep shit anyway. This might be the last one for quite a while."

I won't argue with that.

His teammate didn't argue either. Instead, he dropped into a chair and waved. "Gimme."

While the two soldiers indulged themselves with the ship's booze supply, Syreen sneaked away. Once out of sight, she didn't have to tell them to ignore her.

The skipper's quarters seemed like a good place to relax and calm down. She let herself drop into a chair and took a few deep breaths.

What kind of creature was that? Its mind didn't feel like my People at all, and yet, it had power. Those fangs . . .

Worst, it healed, it almost survived two lethal shots.

It clearly belonged to my dearest foe. It mentioned the master.

What mess did I get myself into?

No.

I didn't start it, but I will clean that shit up. I'll put an end to that mastering.

There was that little problem of getting away from Hawthorne with an AP destroyer watching. She'd have to do something about that.

Syreen strolled up to the captain's seat. He was alone on the bridge. "How did your inspection go?"

"Unpleasant as usual. And for you?" Mo radiated worry.

"Easy. You might miss a bottle or two, though."

"Oh, that's no big deal. The good stuff is safely put away where they'll never find it. But I thought . . ."

"They never laid their hands on me."

"Oh. Okay." He shrugged. "We'll see what happens. They're missing one of their party."

"How's that?"

"No clue. They left one head short. That one must still be aboard."

She gave him a cold smile. "Unless he accidentally

dropped into the converter feed."

The captain's eyes widened. He tried to lean away from her, only his backrest didn't let him. "Got on your bad side, eh?"

"Totally."

"Crap." He waved both hands. "Once their skipper learns about it, we're doomed."

"No, you're not. His boozed-up buddies will take the blame." *At least until their master learns about this event. Thereafter . . .*

She shrugged. "What's the message drone schedule here?"

Mo didn't consult his computer. "Once every tencycle. Hawthorne is quite important."

"Then we'd better leave within the tencycle."

"That bad, ah?"

"We can't know what they will come up with next. Do you want to learn about it?"

"Not the hard way, no." The captain smiled. "I'll keep my business short this time. I'll just check with the guild, and once our provisions are loaded up, we're gone for Gattaca."

After a moment, he added, "I guess you're not interested in another stopover, are you?"

"No."

He pointed at the navigator station. "While I'm gone, feel free to check for a route that suits you best. We always traveled through Grenada, but that's a major fleet base. After our trouble here, it wouldn't be wise to show up there, ah?"

"No."

"We're going through a lot of trouble because of you. But you know what? I don't care. It's time to make a change, and I think you might be the one who can make it happen."

The captain rose and walked out.

Syreen's gaze remained fixed on the door long after he'd left.

CHAPTER TWENTY-ONE

Mo leaned back in his chair and nodded. "Yusef, get *Molly* going while we can."

"Yes, Skipper." The pilot entered a few commands.

The ship trembled once, when her engines came to life, and a second time when the dock clamps released her. Everything was as it should be, but Mo feared trouble.

Yusef had swung the ship around and cleared well away from Hawthorne Orbital when Mo's console indicated an incoming call.

He waited and counted to ten before he opened the line. *"Molly Malone* here. What's up?"

"Hawthorne harbor master John Hogan calling. Upon request from Captain Ogilvy of the AP destroyer Cunning, *all traffic in the Hawthorne system is suspended. You're to return to your dock immediately."*

Mo gave Yusef an encouraging smile and gazed at his passenger. "You can't be serious. I've got a contract and a schedule to keep. I'm already late, and I've got perishable cargo to deliver."

"Molly Malone, I can assure you it is a serious request. I'm not happy about it, either, but I must insist on your returning."

"Hawthorne, I understand you're just the messenger. However, as you know, such changes of schedule are costly. Is that request backed up by any offer of compensation?"

There was a new voice on the line. "Molly Malone, *this is Captain Ogilvy of APS Cunning speaking. I can assure you, my request is backed up by four powerful pulse cannons."*

Mo shook his head. Listening in on a two-way call between harbor and ship already was a breach of common standards. Speaking up uninvited was worse.

He muted his line and turned to Syreen. "So what are we doing now?"

"He can't do anything while docked at the orbital station. Before he can act upon his threat, he must clear away and get a direct line of sight on us—which he currently doesn't have, as the planet is getting between us. Are you willing to hold his bet until he shows his hand?"

"Sounds like a dangerous gamble."

"That's what it is. But his hand is not as good as he thinks."

"So. I'd like to hear more about that, but I fear I must tell him something now."

"Trust me."

He shrugged. "Not that I'd have too many options. Yusef, speed up a bit." He reopened his line. "Captain Ogilvy, by all common standards you're entitled to inspect my ship, and I already honored your authority. However, I don't think you're authorized to suspend general trade, cutting the lifeline of AP research stations dependent on a continuous flow of provisions and sentencing innocent people to hunger, starvation and death. As a merchant known for his honesty and reliability, I must turn down your request for now."

"Merchant skipper, you will cut your engines and await inspection. As you said, I'm entitled to do that."

Mo winked at Syreen. "Sorry, Captain, you're right, you're entitled to do that, but you already did. You cannot twist your authority to turn inspection into a permanent suspension."

"What? Wait until I get you! You will see what I can do with your precious ass!"

He switched to mute again. "This can only get worse."

The Duchy officer nodded. "He's overstepping his authority. I've read AP regulations—he can't shoot you right after an inspection. But that won't stop him. The fear of his superiors comes first, regulations and honor second."

"That's sick."

"Be honest. It sucks."

"Yes. But that doesn't change the situation. We're on the wrong end of four powerful pulse cannons, as our dear Captain Ogilvy so nicely pointed out."

"No. Currently his guns are pointing well away from us."

"They won't remain so."

"No."

She still didn't seem worried.

Strange, but neither am I.

Mo sat down into his chair. "Yusef?"

"They're coming into range around the planet. A centicycle or two, and they can go to full acceleration, or start shooting."

"Okay. Ma'am Fleet Commander in Charge, it's time for a decision. Fold or force showdown?"

"The moment you see their hot guns, you cut your engine. But I don't think that will happen today."

"Yusef, you heard her."

"Prepared, Poppa." Yusef checked his board. "Almost there."

"They'll shoot a warning," Syreen said. "That's in the regulations, too, and I don't think he'll ignore them more than necessary."

"Hot guns," Yusef announced, and cut *Molly's* engines.

His board showed the stray light of interplanetary dust heated up by a near miss.

"Oops," Yusef said.

"Oops," Mo echoed, when his board showed a bright flash where the *Cunning* had been. "What was that?"

"A major reactor failure," Syreen said. "Seems they've overstrained their system. Too bad that their cooling required urgent maintenance."

He stared at her. "And how would you've known about

that?"

"I didn't know. Their inspection team knew. Or, put differently, their inspection team knew this maintenance was due. Too bad, they didn't foresee their captain would immediately venture on a strenuous chase."

"But you did."

"No. I didn't rule out the possibility. However, had Ogilvy played by the Books, he and his crew would still be alive. I'm sorry they had to learn their lesson the hard way."

"Sorry, but not sad."

"No. It's war, and they're the enemy."

Mo studied her face. There wasn't much more to say about it. Or yes, there was. He tapped his board.

"Hawthorne harbor master for *Molly Malone.* I'm sorry to report a major incident that we just recorded. Are you prepared to receive our report?"

The time lag was still short, but noticeable.

"*Molly Malone, we're ready to receive your report. Do you have any clue what might have happened to that unlucky destroyer?*"

Mo glanced at Syreen. "Sorry, no. Only a wild guess—my engineer says it might have been a reactor failure that blew up their ship."

"*That's what our guys say, too. But why?*"

"We're wondering whether the ship was ready to sail. While they were inspecting us, someone mentioned maintenance needs. What if they forgot to keep their captain informed?"

"*Oh my. Poor bastards.*"

"Indeed. Please add our condolences to your report. We're truly sorry it went that way. If they had played by the Books . . ."

"*Yes. Have a smooth journey,* Molly Malone."

CHAPTER TWENTY-TWO

The skipper gazed across his crew and the single passenger in a corner of *Molly's* bridge. "We've reached the Gattaca system. It was a smooth travel indeed. Only six-sigma jumps, across unknown routes, and still faster than any of the beaten tracks. I've never seen or heard of a better navigator."

She smiled at him, confident and not the least embarrassed by his praise.

Mo went on, "The question now, however, is how to proceed. While Gattaca is at the far end of a very long sequence of jumps—which puts a lot of strain on any ship except ours now—message drones run by the hectocycle, nevertheless. It's quite possible they already know about the events at Hawthorne."

Syreen nodded. "We'd better assume they do. However, they can't know the details. They might know we'd been inspected, but then they also know there were no issues. Of course they know this AP ship blew up while we were there. They'll want to know why. So there won't be any trouble until we're docked."

"And once we're docked?"

"If they already got any instructions at all, they'll lock us up until another inspection team arrives."

Mo shook his head. "Why did we come here, then?"

Again, he was amazed by her confident smile.

"Why, we're here to deliver your cargo," she said. "Contracts must be honored."

Yusef waved for attention.

63

Mo turned to his pilot. "Yes?"

"Skipper, there's a warship docked at the station."

"Any details?"

Yusef checked his board. "Frigate. Wasn't here last time, Mo. What does that mean?"

"You remember our first visit, Yusef?"

"Sure, Poppa."

"We met a corvette. They keep a ship here to discourage pirates. Back then, the dock master told me they'd asked for a larger vessel for evacuation purposes, just in case."

"So the station doesn't have more than sixty inhabitants?" Syreen asked. "An AP Gammon-class frigate can be run by a crew of four, but the usual crew size is twelve. Life support systems are certified for seventy-two."

Mo shook his head. "Must be about a hundred people, not counting the entertainers. Forty researchers and assistants, twelve guards, station command and engineering are ten people, and another forty or so service hands."

The fleet commander shook her head, too. "You can overstrain life support by about ten percent for a few jumps, or by thirty percent in an emergency — to reach the next station or planet. But not for the whole way back. We know what that means."

Mo nodded. "Their plans only cover the *important* people."

"That sucks," Yusef commented.

Haiki agreed.

"We're here to do something about that," Syreen said.

"We can't do anything about that if we're locked up," Mo pointed out. *Oh, that smile of hers!*

"I'll do something about that, too."

"You. Alone." He meant to mock her, but she seemed to miss that.

"Yes. I'll clean that cesspit."

"You're talking with confidence."

"You can trust me, like at Hawthorne." She cocked her head. "I'm not sure what to do with you, though. Of course, you can travel on with your *Molly*, but I fear you can't go back to AP territory. Once I'm done here, you'll be high up on their blacklist."

"I'm sure you're right. I knew before Hawthorne we'd face that problem one day. However, I had hoped we could take *Molly* past Gattaca and find some contracts at the borders."

"Where pirates get every third unescorted ship."

"Yeah, we all know that's a pretty rough region."

"Unless you're the pirate." Syreen gave him a stern look. "I couldn't allow that. I shoot pirates."

Mo contemplated that last sentence for a while. The path she'd insinuated had indeed occurred to him. Not because he, still considering himself a more or less honest merchant, was particularly fond of the prospect of capturing other merchants, but because he hadn't been able to come up with any better ideas.

"I have a different offer for you," she said. "Currently, I can't offer you compensation for your *Molly*. Only in the long run we'll see whether I can find a new ship for you. Right now, I can only offer you a job."

"A job? Here?"

"Starting from here, and coming along with me."

"But not aboard *Molly*, from what I understand of your previous statements — what's on your mind?"

She still wore that confident smile, but now with an impish twitch in the corners of her mouth.

"You'd have to learn how to run a frigate."

CHAPTER TWENTY-THREE

Syreen retreated into a corner of Molly's bridge. *Ignore me. For now, forget about me.*

Yusef was busy steering the ship into the docking clamps, while Haiki checked the readings of the freight bays. Mo acknowledged another incoming call.

"Molly Malone, *stand by for an inspection team and hold your bill of freight ready.*"

"Yes, sure, we're gathered on the bridge."

"That would be?"

"Yusef, my pilot, Haiki, my engineer, and myself."

"No one else?"

"A load of frosties. They won't cause you trouble."

"You didn't pick up passengers?"

"I didn't bring any passengers along. I know your rules."

"Well then. I'll be right there."

She waited until the inspection team arrived, and sneaked out before the door closed behind the illustrious group—Gattaca's dock master, station commander, and chief of guard together with the captain of *APS Bumblebee*. She'd meet them later, after the inspection.

Two guards in AP marine infantry uniform paraded their boredom before the airlock. She felt into their minds and found the usual inclination for abuse of power, probably a recruiting requirement for AP bullies. *Enemy.*

Biting them served two purposes—first, it weakened them to the point where they wouldn't cause her any trouble even without mind control for the next few cycles. Second, she'd need every bit of power to bring the rest of the station under her control.

When she passed the dockside door, she smiled, both for the cameras and the third guard waiting there.

"Hey! Who are you? Wait, what—"

She leaned over him as if to kiss him. When he felt her fangs sink into his skin, it was too late. Her beast cheered.

The station's klaxons summoned the remaining eight guards to her court. They had no more chance to resist her will than the team of sauroids on Appalahoo she had commanded to take one big monster down, and this time, she didn't take all their blood. Instead, she urged them forward to the frigate dock.

As Syreen had expected, the frigate had its own guards on duty. As she had feared, these two weren't easy to control and each got one shot off before she could will them under her command. The response fire of her own escort made them rethink and gave her the necessary time to conquer their minds.

Again, she drained them of their blood, but only after her small party had entered the frigate. She left two guards behind at the airlock.

The young lieutenant holding the bridge was unable to cope with the situation. When she entered, followed by two AP marines, he froze, stammered something incomprehensible, and almost wet his pants.

"I am Syreen, Duchy Fleet Commander in Charge. Lieutenant, regard your ship as captured. Call your crew to the bridge. Make clear that I will not tolerate any signs of disrespect or resistance."

Calm down and act.

"Crew, proceed to the bridge. Crew, proceed to the bridge." He paused. "Crew, *APS Bumblebee* is under enemy command. You're ordered to refrain from any hostile action."

That wasn't exactly what I asked for, Syreen mused.

She focused on the lieutenant. *Freeze. Don't move.*

Two of her guards remained with the officer. Syreen and four more moved to gather the crew.

Her senses told her where to look for crew members, and her mental orders prevented them from doing any mischief, even without direct sight. She could have ordered them to come, but by collecting them the conventional way, she could maintain a pretense of normality, easing her mental commands.

The outcome was the same—the entire crew with the exception of their captain was lined up on the bridge.

"I am Syreen, Duchy Fleet Commander in Charge. Your ship is my prize, and you are my prisoners."

"This is piracy," an aged noncommissioned officer wearing an engineer's badge muttered.

"This is war," she corrected. "Without advance declaration of war, the Association attacked my planet, causing massive civil casualties. I will not hold you personally responsible for any crimes of war committed there, but you must understand that you cannot expect me to go easy on you. Your situation is this—I will take your ship, and I cannot afford to take any prisoners along. You have two choices—you can stay behind on Gattaca on parole, or you can demand execution. Which is it?"

"What does this parole mean?" asked the engineer.

"You can look it up in your own regulations. In essence, you're supposed to refrain from any hostile action. Should you violate the terms of parole as laid down in your Books, you cannot demand prisoner of war treatment. Put differently, you'd be no better than a pirate."

The senior noncom swallowed hard. "Boys, you'd better read the Books first. I choose parole."

No surprise, the other crew members followed suit.

APS Bumblebee was hers.

A flash at her desk announced an incoming call.

"*Bumblebee*, captain speaking," she said.

"*What's this nonsense? You'd better surrender right now, or I'll have your ass flogged with a steel wire. I'm Captain Hardcastle, and I'll have my ship back.*"

"Captain Hardcastle, your threat of undue treatment has been recorded. I'm not impressed, though. The *Bumblebee* is no longer your ship, and I needn't remind you it's the only warship in this system."

"*This is outrageous! You – you pirate!*"

"Captain Hardcastle, I'm Duchy Fleet Commander in Charge, and since the Association attacked my planet, we're at war."

There was a pause. "*I have the crew of your ship.*"

"Captain Hardcastle, the independent merchant *Molly Malone* has never been my ship. I've merely been a blind passenger. Regarding her crew, I assume you didn't intend to imply anything like taking civil merchants hostage, which would be an act of piracy by your own regulations and would be treated as such."

Again, there was a pause, followed by a new voice.

"*Bumblebee, I'm Major Baker, commandant of Gattaca station. It is my duty to request you to surrender to my guards and return control of AP frigate* Bumblebee *to its rightful captain.*"

"Major Baker, I understand your obligation, but I must respectfully refuse your request. *Bumblebee* is my prize, rightfully captured under terms of war."

"*What do you expect to gain from that? You can't get away from Gattaca. Our station is well armed.*"

"Major, I'm aware of your armament. However, as long as my frigate is close to its dock, it's out of your line of fire, while I can train its guns on your station anytime."

"*You wouldn't shoot on a civil station.*"

"Major, I wouldn't shoot on a station behaving like a civil

station. However, you just issued a threat against my ship, so I have to consider your station as military and hostile. There's no way back. I have no choice but to shoot your station. I don't want any civilian collateral damage, so I propose you move your staff aboard *Molly Malone*. I will give you four cycles."

"The AP will hold you accountable for that."

"You have an evacuation to organize now, Major. Don't waste time. I will not extend my deadline."

"You wouldn't . . ." His voice trailed off.

"Major, I give you an advance warning and sufficient time to get away. That's more than the AP fleet gave my people before they shot our orbital station with thousands of civilians out of space. You could say, Admiral Cornelius Ravenport of *APS Illustrious* established the rules for this conflict, and I'm bending them in your favor."

"Ravenport. That explains a lot. Okay, I get your point. I'm sure we can meet your deadline. I'll call you again when we're ready."

Don't play tricks on me, Syreen thought, but didn't voice it. He was cooperative. No need to trigger his defiance—or his imagination.

70

CHAPTER TWENTY-FOUR

Syreen watched her plot and sighed. Major Baker tried a nasty trick, or perhaps it had been Captain Hardcastle's idea. A shuttle had left the station. It was now dropping toward Gattaca's surface.

A wave of fear came from that shuttle, and some of these emotions were familiar—Mo, Yusef and Haiki were aboard.

She didn't intervene. She had to guard her ship.

Those poor souls had to live with their fear, as she had to live with knowing about it.

For now.

Two cycles later, the shuttle returned. Her deadline was almost over. A few moments passed, enough for the shuttle crew to cover the distance from shuttle dock to *Molly's* dock running, and then the big merchant ship slowly sailed away from the station.

The expected call followed suit.

Syreen sighed again before accepting the call.

"*Bumblebee, this is Major Baker again. We've vacated the station. You may have noticed the shuttle—some of our guests preferred to stay instead of traveling with us. Remaining on the station was out of the question, so we sent them dirtside.*"

"Major Baker, I strongly doubt they made this choice voluntarily."

"*This is your personal opinion.*"

She issued a few commands on her panel. "Indeed, for now it is. Once I'm finished here, I will collect evidence and record witness statements, though."

"Do as you like. We're departing now."

"Given you told me the truth, I wish you easy jumps."

"Have your fun."

His sarcasm was lost on her. She rose and walked back and forth between the stations, trying to keep an eye on everything. *Bumblebee* undocked, sailed clear from the station and turned its bow toward the nearest gun turret—which began to train on her, as she had expected.

Syreen shot first. Together with the gun turret, a large part of the station disappeared in a cloud of debris.

Hard acceleration drove *Bumblebee* backward, away from the station. There was no time to waste—as she had expected, only two centicycles later, the station blew up.

Thank you for doing my work. Bastards.

Unless *Molly* had brought one, the explosion had deprived her of the only shuttle in this system capable of going dirtside.

Surely Baker and Hardcastle were cheering now, even if their latest trick had failed to damage the frigate.

Time for my own trick.

Frigates carried only that kind of small shuttles needed to transfer a boarding party from one ship to another. Those little scooters weren't meant to travel into a planetary gravity sink.

Frigates weren't meant to do that, either, but according to the ship's technical manuals, they were certified to dive into a not-too-dense gas environment. If Syreen could do it with a corvette, she could do it with a frigate, too, so that was what she did.

The approach required care—atmospheric currents, gravity and momentum had to be kept in balance—and patience. Breaking the only ship available for rescue wouldn't help anyone.

What makes this maneuver hard is the uncertainty. Will I find anyone to rescue once I arrive at the surface? I don't even know if they're still alive now!

Another call.

"What's up now?"

"You can't take the frigate dirtside!" Baker yelled.

"No need to shout. I read you loud and clear. You'll see, I'll take her down in one piece. Don't worry."

"No, you don't understand — you can't bring an interstellar vessel into reach of the genex!"

Genex? That's what they call the locals? Ah, genetic experiments, right.

"As you didn't leave me an intact shuttle, I have to. Perhaps you should have considered that."

Just in time, she let *Bumblebee* sway to one side, before a strong downward gust could take her off her course. *How did I know about that gust?*

"Let's talk about that."

"No talks. I must navigate a ship now. Bye."

She cut the line and focused on her task. Friction caused the hull to heat up — she had to decelerate further.

CHAPTER TWENTY-FIVE

Touchdown. *Bumblebee* came to a rest on her belly. Syreen took a deep breath and leaned back.

Being gentle with such a huge metal body was hard work. Finding a place to set it down had been even harder — on the almost even rock surface marked as shuttle landing pad by countless scratches, the frigate might have started rolling around.

The mental emanations of her crew and the defrosted girls were moving against the planetary rotation anyway, so she had followed and passed over them.

Come to me. It wouldn't help if she allowed them to be scared away by the noise of a few crushing trees and scrubs.

A few computer commands secured the frigate. She'd have to invite those people in, but couldn't let them mess around with *Bumblebee's* controls.

When she finally opened the outer airlock, they were already close.

"Over here!" she called.

Mo came around a group of trees and staggered. "Syreen, is that you?"

"That's me, myself, and I, yes."

He regained his balance, made some quick steps forward, and noticed the huge body. "Bugger me. That's impossible."

Mo closed the distance, pulled her close and hugged her. "Whatever. I'll take a miracle if I get one. It's still unbroken, is it?"

"I'm a Navigator. I don't break my own ship."

74

"Of course. But you could've come by shuttle."

"There was none. They blew up the station."

Now he radiated amusement while trying to keep a stern face. "So you took a frigate dirtside."

"So I took my frigate dirtside to pick you up."

Mo waved his crewmates and a flock of scarcely dressed young women closer. "You know, that's the kind of actions that can get you deep into trouble. It's also that kind of actions that makes people want to follow you to hell and back — because they start believing you *can* come back."

"Been there, done that."

"You mean that dreadnaught?"

"No. I mean being imprisoned on Nysa Four, questioned by their overlord, educated by his most skilled torturer, then escaping in one piece." She waved. "Let's not take that topic any deeper. Get aboard and make yourself comfortable. I have to collect a few more AP victims."

"Who do you mean?"

"The previous entertainment team."

"They're genex prey. That's dangerous."

"It's worse for them."

"Isn't your mission too important to risk your life?"

"I'm not risking my life, and this is my mission." She smiled at the women. "There will be no more abuse. Be nice to each other."

One of them found the courage to ask, "Who are you?"

"I'm Syreen."

"Why are you doing this?"

"Because I can."

"Why? What makes you think you can fight the entire AP?"

"I'm a Navigator."

"That doesn't make you special."

"But it does. Navigator with a capital N. It's more than a

job description."

"Capital letters don't win battles."

"But Navigators do. Mo can tell you what I told him. That must suffice for now."

CHAPTER TWENTY-SIX

Leaving *Bumblebee* and her noisy passengers behind, Syreen could start listening to Gattaca. Not just the star singing its lonesome lament—the planet was echoing the rhythm, adding its own vibrations to the tune.

She'd been dirtside before, but she hadn't noticed such delicate details until now. Perhaps this kind of perception took some getting used to?

There was no basis for comparison—and yet, the song told so much, of spin and tumble, continental drift and friction, convectional streams, magnetic field patterns, of conglomerates and erosion . . .

She called herself to order. *Only the surface counts now.*

Her experience with surface dwellers—plants and wildlife—was limited. However, those few encounters had been a tough school. How many space jockeys would survive a sauroid fight on Appalahoo?

Bare-handedly.

Syreen had reason to feel confident. Whatever Gattaca tossed in her way, she should be able to handle it.

The trees and scrubs grew far less densely than on Appalahoo, and so far there were no deep footprints or other indicators of big predators, or of large animals at all.

Syreen picked up two leaves. The shapes were different. A circle with a little tip the one, a seven-fingered hand the other. There had to be a reason, only she couldn't figure it out. *Not enough data.*

She moved on, following a hint of human despair still in

the far distance. As long as she could follow this trace, she wouldn't arrive too late.

Yet, I'm running out of time. They're *running out of time.*

Wet drops covered her bare skin. First, only a few, but soon they came in numbers.

Oh great, another planet with broken plumbing.

She glanced at her feet. *Getting wet isn't the worst. Now the dirt clogs to my boots.*

The dirt on her boots wasn't the worst, either, she recognized when a long, sharp object dug deep into her left side. Pain made her drop on her knees. Her vision turned dark.

No.

The beast opened her mind first, then her eyes. Five strong mental auras of a new, yet unknown and thus unnoticed species promised sources of power in easy reach.

They radiated mental power, too—a kind of subliminal command to ignore them and sleep, which her beast had already neutralized.

One of them still clung to the stick in her side with its four hands. Aside from this oddity, the creature was human-like, with two feet, one quite large sexual organ—erect?—and a scaled brown skin.

When a long, forked tongue whipped in her direction, she glanced up and smiled.

Well aware of four more creatures with four more sharp-pointed sticks, she slowly rose to her feet.

Freeze. You are mine.

Unlike her, they were unable to resist her mental command.

With little effort she pulled the primitive weapon out. Some blood followed, but the deep wound closed quickly.

Her attackers watched in horror as she healed and bared her fangs. They weren't allowed to run nor to fight back. They could only watch as she consumed them one after the other.

In the end, she licked her lips. A pity she had no time to waste. Sampling one of those big cocks could've been fun.

Next time, perhaps.

Only a little itch in Syreen's side reminded her of the stab she had suffered, plus the dried corpses of five locals—five genetic experiments, results of an outrageous crime against humanity, but still nutritious for her.

They had paid the highest price for their attack. Syreen refused to feel bad about it. Given the choice of avoiding contact at all, attempting communication, or seeking a fight, they'd gambled too high.

It was the natural way—survival of the fittest. Civilization could overcome some of this principle's disadvantages. Civilization required abstaining from stabbing each other, though.

Her beast got along well with the natural way, and she fully agreed. Cooperation was good, and if that didn't work, winning a fight was second best.

Poor bastards.

Now that Syreen knew what to feel for, the locals wouldn't take her by surprise again. Just the opposite—accumulations of their mental auras gave the locals' habitations away, and merged into one of those, not too far away, she sensed her frightened targets.

Hang in there, I'm coming.

There was no way to go faster—she still had to be watchful while negotiating her way across roots, fallen logs, broken branches, through scratchy scrubs and around large trees.

More locals roamed the area between her and her destination. She didn't want to sacrifice them all to her beast, but she couldn't allow them to block her escape route, either.

Come to me.

She made them break their sticks' sharp tips and wait for

her bite. Taking only some of their blood weakened but wouldn't kill them, and provided her with again more mental power.

Sleep.

Five more groups of locals were put to sleep before Syreen deemed the area clear and continued her approach.

Now came the most dangerous part — could she deceive an entire habitation full of hostile locals? Her tricks had worked on warship crews, orbital stations, and planetary bases, but she expected trouble and was prepared for it.

Whatever the locals had done to their involuntary human guests, she hadn't come to repay in kind. Cruelty or unprovoked violence didn't become a Duchy Fleet Commander in Charge. Most importantly, she hadn't come to commit genocide.

That was why she hadn't brought a gun.

CHAPTER TWENTY-SEVEN

So far, *Ignore me* had worked fine for Syreen.

Now she faced a primitive cage, large enough to hold eleven scared women, locked with primitive bolts. Every inmate could've opened it easily, if it weren't for the guards.

Four locals kept their eyes on the cage and the naked women inside, occasionally rattled the bars with their sharp sticks' blunt end or presented huge erections to the captives.

There seemed to be a simple and obvious explanation for the situation. The women had volunteered as entertainers for the orbital research station—with a sexual connotation—and were now held captive as sex slaves. Except for the accommodation, not much had changed.

The clients were different, but their cocks were not. So, how bad was it?

Twelve entertainers had arrived at Gattaca. Now there were eleven women. One was missing. Why, since when?

I'll ask the others later. If they're able to talk about it.

Judging by their current attitude, they knew, but wouldn't want to think about it.

That bad, huh?

She focused on the closest guard. *Come to me.*

One after another, she took blood, power, and knowledge. The habitation offered shelter to about as many families as one had fingers at his hands, and a family had as many members. That was the limit, that was the law. If a woman was with child, and her family was full, mother and child were killed. Thus, women in full families weren't eager to breed. If

81

the males needed stress relief, they had to take a woman of another clan. Their males might retaliate in kind, and males would die, making room for children. That was the way of life—except in this clan. Slaves didn't count as family. Slave women could be taken. Newborn children, if any, were killed, even the girls, as they weren't worth the effort of feeding them until they were old enough to be useful.

Nice people. Nice manners. Matching this nice planet. Even worse with their mental powers—I can understand why Baker feared my bringing a frigate down into their reach.

Can I blame them for what they are? Can I condemn them? No, I can't. They're using damaged goods—people with only two arms—but working genitals to reduce their need to make war, to the greater good of their clan. This may be perfectly legal within their own jurisdiction, even if they don't know that term yet.

I can condemn those who sent the women down here, though.

And I can object against keeping them locked up.

Leave us alone.

The last thought was directed at the guards. Next, Syreen focused on the captives. With a finger on her lips, she commanded, *You're exempt from ignoring my presence now.*

The storm of feelings almost overwhelmed her. Surprise, fear, disbelief, but also hope—so they hadn't given up yet?

"I am Syreen," she said very slowly and opened the cage. "Come or stay, it's your choice."

"Come where?" one red-haired woman dared to ask.

"To my ship and off-planet. I cannot offer you safety, not yet, but I can promise you better than this."

"You have a ship?"

"I've captured an AP frigate. Stolen. Now come. The guards will return."

Without looking back, she turned and walked off toward her ship. When she sensed the women hurrying to follow, she allowed herself a contented smile.

A half cycle later, Syreen sensed the redhead closing up.

"Syreen, this forest looks all the same to me. How can you tell where we're going? I'm feeling lost."

"I'm a Navigator. Navigators don't get lost."

"Okay — but how? Did you leave traces on your way in?"

Syreen looked down. "I should have, but the precipitation washed it all away."

"How do you know, then?"

"I'm listening to the planet's song. It tells me all I need to know."

Redhead pouted, but didn't ask more.

Not counting the occasional *Ouch* upon stepping on something sharp or pointy with their bare feet, the women remained silent. Only when the frigate's slender body came into view did they begin to cheer.

Syreen led them to the airlock, where some of the newly arrived *entertainers* took care of their predecessors. They held medipacs and cups with hot forwine ready, and it wasn't entirely clear which was appreciated more.

Mo appeared. "I allowed them access to our provisions. The ship's well stocked, so this little party won't hurt."

"Sure."

"Sorry. I didn't mean to challenge your command, but I thought you might need help with the administrative stuff."

"I'm glad you're here with me, Mo. It's hard enough to fly that ship — it's impossible to take care of the passengers in addition. I'd really appreciate if you could assume command on all things internal, so I can focus on navigation."

Mo mocked a salute. "Yessir."

She smiled.

"Okay. Let the women take care of themselves, and I'll get us away from here."

"Did you have any trouble with the locals?"

"Not much." Her side still itched, but perhaps she was just

nervous. "I couldn't find the last one. I fear she's dead."

"Most likely, as an example for the others. Yusef can assist you—he's on the bridge."

"Yes, thanks. Tell our guests it may be a bit bumpy until we reach open space."

"Okay."

Syreen didn't look forward to the climb. Hard work and no fun.

Yusef welcomed her on the bridge and quickly cleared the pilot seat.

She nodded, sat down, and began the unlock sequence. Of course, she hadn't left *Bumblebee's* flight controls open for everyone.

"Anything I can do for you?" Yusef asked.

"Yes. Please watch the long-distance sensors and the radio. I need to know about new visitors—everything else should have time until we've reached open space."

"Sure."

She checked the system anyway.

Major Baker had cheated her, as she had known—the entertainers hadn't volunteered to go dirtside. Now that she had proof, *Molly Malone's* head start had grown too comfortable, though. She couldn't afford breaking her frigate in a futile attempt to catch up.

So there was no need to hurry skyward.

"I didn't know this type was built for dirtside operations," Yusef said.

"It isn't."

"But—"

"But we're here. I brought her down, and I'll take her up in one piece. Don't worry."

"I won't worry. I like to see you doing magic. Sometimes I wish I could do it, too."

"I'll teach you some of it. Later. During the climb, I must focus on what I'm doing. You may watch, but I can't answer questions."

"Okay. Difficult magic. I'll shut up."

Indeed, he kept silent while she cautiously lifted *Bumblebee* from the ground. The ship took up a little speed and rose toward a cloudy cover.

That was the easy part.

Strong gusts began to tear at the frigate. Syreen tried to keep the ship on its course and almost despaired.

Fool.

Fool that I am.

I just have to get up and out, no matter where.

So she allowed *Bumblebee* to follow and ride the wind as it came. From there on, she could significantly reduce her efforts.

That's some kind of un-navigating. Giving up so much control is unnerving. I don't want to get used to it.

CHAPTER TWENTY-EIGHT

Mo shook his head. "I can't answer your questions, sorry. I'm as clueless as you are."

He gazed at the faces in *Bumblebee's* mess, some grim, some only worried. Some of the women were holding tight to each other, some were leaning back in their chairs with crossed arms.

"See, I'm a—I was an independent merchant, hauling goods around. I've done the trip to Gattaca a few times before, ignoring what I saw and heard. I knew something was wrong. I shouldn't have brought any of you here, and I'm truly sorry."

"Sorry my ass," Jona said. "You made good money delivering us to this cesspit."

Mo sighed. "You're right. I don't want to fool you. I knew something was very fishy. I knew I never had to take any passengers back from Gattaca. I told myself I didn't know anything for sure—which is true, but still I've done wrong."

He pointed at the forward bulkhead. "She showed me my wrongs. She took action where I should have, to change things. Now things have changed. Gattaca Orbital doesn't exist anymore. No more abuse of women, no more women sent dirtside as sex slaves for violent locals. Ask around what you've missed."

Some of the women he'd brought on this last trip looked into the faces of the women Syreen had rescued. Most of their scars were now covered by spare AP uniforms from the frigate's storage, but their faces still showed the pain they had suffered.

"Believe me, I'm grateful," ginger Gwen said.

The merchant nodded. Her statement sounded sarcastic to him. "Yes, true, you're out of job. No credits for the time you spent on your trip, no credits for entertainment here—no compensation for the mistreatments. Don't ask me—I just lost my ship, and who knows if and when I can tap my accounts again."

"But what's next?" Jona asked. "Where do we go?"

Their current commandant's arrival spared him an answer he couldn't give. With a serene smile, the *Navigator*—whatever that term should imply—passed round the tables and arrived next to his chair.

"Yes, that's the question, isn't it?" she began. "One thing's for sure. I won't take you to Nysa."

A few women laughed.

"Believe me—whatever happened to you on this cursed planet is a breeze against what I'd face if the AP could get me. I won't go back there—nor to any planet under their control. However, that puts forward the question of where I *could* go, considering their current attitude toward smaller independent star nations. I daresay there's hardly any civilized system on this side of the galaxy I could safely approach. Mo, any ideas?"

He shook his head. "You've pretty much summed it up."

"I feared as much. Okay, you all might ask yourself why and how I got into this mess. I could easily have skipped Gattaca and left you alone. Some of you may be glad I didn't, some probably haven't entirely realized what I saved you from, but that doesn't matter. What matters to you is that I decided to end this kind of abuse, that I made your fate part of my mission—which is to defeat the current AP and teach them proper behavior. The lessons will be hard. I'm talking about war. Let me introduce myself properly. I'm Syreen, and

I'm Fleet Commander in Charge of a one-star nation called the Duchy, the navy of which has been wiped out by the AP—all except for me."

Mo already knew that part.

"In return, I've wiped out one of their dreadnaughts single-handedly, stolen one of their corvettes—an even smaller warship than this one—and successfully fought several more ships of their navy. Thereafter, I traveled to their central planet to find out what they're actually after. I was caught and tortured, but I found out before I left. It's me they're after."

"You," he echoed. "You mean they're starting a war over a single woman? Sorry, Captain, no offense meant."

"No offense taken. Ladies and gentlemen, you must understand my situation in order to understand your situation. You're stuck with me for the moment, and you must know why that might not change for a while. Believe me, I'd really like to take you to a peaceful holiday location where you can pick any job to your liking or marry one of the thousands of rich men roaming around there—you get the picture. Right now, I can't. The only thing I can offer you is the relative safety of my ship—you're guests, not ship's cats, and it's your decision what you do or don't with my male crew. If you have any doubts, questions, or complaints, ask me. Remember, I came to change things."

Mo focused on Haiki. His engineer nodded. He seemed to have understood the implications.

Syreen continued, "I must apologize to my crew, too. I didn't ask them to support my cause, I didn't offer them much of a choice. Worse, my actions cost them their ship."

"We got a fast frigate in exchange," Mo argued. However, he'd already begun to miss his good old *Molly Malone*. He'd been his own boss.

"Are we going to battle?" Jona asked.

"Not if I can avoid it," Syreen replied. "If necessary, I will

fight, and I can assure you I know how to improve my odds —
but any fight would mean the AP found us, and I don't want
them to know where I am."

"Why do they want you?" Gwen asked.

"I know some things no one else knows. Here and now, I
won't change that. You don't need to know. You need to
know, however, that they want me desperately. They'll do
everything to get me. They'll do everything to get answers out
of anyone who could know anything about me. And after-
ward, they'll make sure that anyone can't talk to anyone else.
Clear?"

"Sounds like we'd almost be better off with those four-
armed bastards," Gwen said, but she smiled. "Almost."

Jona shook her head. "No. Sounds like we're better off if
we stay close to her. So far, the AP lost a dreadnaught, a corvette, a frigate, and an orbital station, and this woman is alive
and ready to kick their cursed asses again. Looks like a bright
future."

"I couldn't have put it better." Syreen gazed around. "I'd
gladly have dropped you in a civilized, nice place like Kyris,
but you wouldn't be safe there. Instead, I'll take you to a few
of the most remote places you could imagine where we'll
meet a few friends — and then, I indeed plan to kick some
more ass. Until then, I must ask for your patience and cooperation."

"Cooperation?" Jona asked.

"In keeping my ship clean and tidy."

"Oh — don't worry, we know to behave. No need to put us
in the fridge again." Jona bit her lip and plucked at her sleeve.
"This ain't the most comfortable garment — are we required to
wear it at all times?"

"No. No dress code aboard." Syreen waved at Haiki and
Mo. "However, you should ask them what they're willing to
tolerate."

With these girls, I'd tolerate a lot, Mo thought. *No doubt, Haiki and Yusef won't object, either. However, we all know where that will lead.*

Jona put up a mischievous smile. "You mean, if I'm looking for someone to keep me warm at night, I may go nude?"

Oh, what am I worrying about?

CHAPTER TWENTY-NINE

Mo recognized Syreen's request, nudged Haiki, and followed her back to the bridge, where Yusef cleared the pilot seat for her and lined up with them.

What now? lingered in the air between them, unspoken.

She remained standing next to her board. "I already told you, our destination is a very remote location. I haven't picked a route yet, but it will take us at least twenty jumps, perhaps twenty-five, to get there. These jumps will be as smooth as I can make them, but I still don't know whether *Bumblebee* will hold out. Haiki, do you have any clue how good she is?"

"No, captain. I didn't have time for a thorough inspection yet."

"Let me put the question differently. If you'd enter a fellow merchant's ship, could you tell whether it's in better or worse shape than your *Molly?*"

"Uh—yes, I'd say. There are always neglected corners, but you know, the parts that count, hatches, vents, controls, are usually kept tidy. If those are in very good shape, the ship usually is, too. If those are worn or patched together, the maintenance budget must be thin."

"Okay, and if you apply the same criteria to this frigate?"

He considered her idea.

Mo smiled inwardly. Haiki was a good man—he had kept Molly in good shape for many winters without wasting money on extravagances.

Haiki nodded. "It's sub-par even for a merchant, clearly

91

not up to military standards. I'd say, it's been on low maintenance for a long time. However, crucial stuff like airlocks and life support seem to be okay. The provisions are okay, too. My guess is—as the ship was mainly kept for an unlikely evac situation, they made sure it could reach Hawthorne safely, but they didn't care about keeping it battle-ready."

"What would that tell you about its emitters?"

"I'd have to have a look, but as there was no wear while the ship was docked, the emitters should be fine—as they were when the ship was brought here. They should be virtually fresh from maintenance, but I'll check that."

"Do that. From what I could feel until now, there are no jitters. We'll know more after our first jump. What do you think of life support?"

"Uh—when you took us aboard, I checked the converters first. The ladies had their emergency needs, you know? That's the one thing that works really fine—I guess the navy people didn't like failures there, either, as they had their quarters aboard the ship. That should be the last thing we need to worry about."

"What about provisions?"

"Oh, uh, they're equipped to feed a crew of twelve for a kilocycle. We're twenty-seven people—twenty-three passengers and the four of us, and the emergency provisions were meant to feed seventy-two people until Hawthorne—for another twenty tencycles at max. That makes roughly two-and-a-half thousand rations—should be sufficient for about one kilocycle for us."

"Which gives us four tencycles per jump," Syreen calculated.

Mo shook his head. "That's too tight. We need to recharge regularly, which will cost us some tencycles each time, and we already need a tencycle or two between jumps."

She smiled at him. "Yes, I know the Books. I will recharge

at least after each sequence of jumps, but I plan to do multiple jumps in quick succession. There's no need to stay close to stars that can't feed us."

"Multiple jumps *will* put strain on the emitters," Haiki said. "They might overheat, and that causes wear."

"I know. After all, I'm a *Navigator*."

Mo still wondered why she stressed that term. Oh, she was good—the best he ever heard of—but she might as well call herself *pilot*.

Her next statement caught him on the wrong foot.

"Overheating is no issue on seven-sigma jumps, though."

CHAPTER THIRTY

Syreen had expected arguments, but not Mo's violent denial. "No!" he roared. "Nobody does seven-sigma. That's nonsense. Impossible."

After a moment of staring at each other, he calmed down and continued, "Sorry, gal—but that must stop. We can't risk our lives with such foolishness. Please, get back to reality. I know you're a good pilot, and I understand that you're under pressure, but that's no excuse for gambling."

She nodded and stepped back from her station.

"Okay. Come over and check this jump solution. Yusef, you, too."

With a mixture of hesitation, curiosity, and reserve, they leaned over her screens.

"Another new route?" Yusef asked. "Where no one has gone before?"

She nodded. "Where the AP won't find us."

"Looks like a smooth jump," Mo said. "Let me see—that's a—*seven?*"

Yusef glanced at Mo, at Syreen, at the screen again, and shook his head. "I didn't know navy computers could compute this."

"They can't," she said. "I must admit I had to enhance our software first."

Mo stared at her. "You fiddled with our software?"

She stared back. "I did, and that's not the first time. Before you object, I must tell you about a merchant with a wiped-out library. Her name was *Mary Of Skye* — "

Mo interrupted her. "I've heard about that ship. Her pilot left the ship on Woo, but only after leaving a little bug in the computer. Had everything worked as planned, no one would have learned about it, but *Mary Of Skye* was lucky — they managed to fix their data, and along the way they saved a miner's life. On Mongo, they reported their former pilot, and now the entire galaxy knows the story." He made a grim face. "No one will ever hire him, or even take him as passenger. He'll probably clean the sewers dirtside for the rest of his miserable life. What was I about to say? Oh, about that merchant — they were saved by a miracle, a one-in-a-billion chance. You shouldn't bet on such odds, gal."

"I admit, seven-sigma is two in a billion, but on her way via Moria Six — the mining colony — to Mongo, *Mary Of Skye* did four seven-sigma jumps in a row."

"What are you talking about? There are no seven-sigma jumps. And what do you know about that lucky ship?"

"More than I will tell you. Only three things — *I'm* the pilot who took her from Woo to Mongo, I taught her computer seven-sigma jumps, and I reconstructed her star library."

"Even if you sound very convincing, that's impossible."

"Speak it out loud. It's inhuman."

Mo stepped backward and eyed her from head to foot. "Sorry for stating the obvious, but you're looking very human to me."

"I thought the same for most of my life, Mo. But when it comes to navigation, my skills can't be explained by the stuff my teachers told me."

"So you're a natural. That still doesn't explain how you can rebuild a star library — if you really did it."

"What else?"

"You could have known about that pilot — you could have brought a new library."

"Oh." Syreen shook her head. "I didn't, but that's indeed a

much simpler explanation."

"It's the only meaningful one. How else would you rebuild a star library?"

Bonehead. No, he just wants a conclusive explanation — and I can give him one. "After you did a jump, how do you know you've arrived at the right system?"

"From the jump parameters—the computer knows . . ." Mo's voice trailed off.

"Come on, you know what I mean. Yusef, any idea?"

"We do an initial scan and check if everything looks as expected. The computer does it."

"And how does the computer do that check?"

Yusef began to grin. "By collecting scan data and comparing it with the library." He turned to Mo. "By building a second library of the local system, so to speak, and comparing that."

Syreen gave him a thumbs up. "Right—it's not just the local system, though. The computer also compares constellations of the nearest stars around plus the landmark ones. Do you know why?"

"No."

"That's one thing my teachers told me. There used to be beacons in many civilized systems, telling new arrivals where they were. But during past wars, beacons were reprogrammed to confuse arriving enemy forces. Beacons were destroyed, beacons could be broken. Navies and merchants began to rely on their own data instead of trusting poorly maintained beacons. That method works even in systems without beacons, it works fine, so why bother to maintain beacons at all? Nowadays, that method is so sophisticated that you can indeed use it to build a star library—that's exactly what explorers do. Of course, you can't build an entire library from the observations of one system, and the ordinary computer doesn't work that way, but in principle, it's possible—if you already know where you are and can help the computer sort

96

things out. That's what I did."

Yusef frowned. "It's not that easy."

"No. It's just a very brief summary of what I really did. I had to double-check all incoming data and add the necessary metadata from my memory—I always memorize the route I'm about to fly, usually for several jumps ahead."

Mo waved. "The jump routes—merchant ships aren't equipped to gather all the data for the jumps. There's more in the library than our scanners can see."

"Of course. That's why we use the library. There are hidden dangers our scanners won't detect—but once you know a route is fine, you can make a safe bet that such obstacles won't appear out of nowhere."

"So it's a very good memory rather than magic," Mo said and nodded. "Okay. I can live with that."

"But you still don't buy my seven-sigma jumps. So, there's only one way—I'll have to demonstrate it."

"You'd have to calculate a new one—we're already past the jump point for your solution."

"Indeed. Check our current position."

Syreen watched Yusef and Mo and waited.

Yusef noticed it first. "We're no longer in the Gattaca system!"

"Correct. We reached the jump point and jumped."

"But I didn't feel anything."

"You shouldn't. After all, it was a seven-sigma jump, and we were busy discussing the library issue."

CHAPTER THIRTY-ONE

Inside Mo, anger and fascination fought a lonely fight. How could she dare to jump so recklessly, without supervision, with untested modifications to the computer? On the other hand, how could one do a jump so smooth that not even he, a seasoned merchant skipper, would sense it happening?

Not fair, he decided. The jump hadn't happened without supervision. Three qualified people had watched the board. And if she had spoken the truth, her modifications had been tested before — only not on this ship.

Fascination won.

"You're surely the best navigator I ever met — probably the best in this sector of our galaxy at all."

"As far as I know, I'm the best all over this galaxy."

From her mouth, it sounded like simply stating a fact, not like boasting.

"How can you be so sure?"

"Because the stars are lonely. They haven't met anyone like me for many megacycles."

"Huh?"

"That's what their songs are telling me."

"Gal, you're crazy."

"Yes. Now, let's return to the business. We had been discussing our route, when we were distracted by this little seven-sigma topic. I assume you take that as a given now? Thanks. We still have a long way to go, and we're a bit short regarding provisions. We'll need to resupply. Where?"

Mo shook his head again. "You think you can arrive at

some system in a stolen ship and go shopping?"

"I know it's not that easy. It won't work everywhere—certainly not in a system where we meet other AP warships. But this is not a stolen ship. It's a ship won in war, and we're already emitting the appropriate transponder code of a Duchy Fleet frigate."

"Okay—it's not stolen. But it's operating far away from its territory."

"It's not that unusual, especially for ships built for escort purposes. I think merchants usually don't complain about piracy protection."

Mo paused. "You have a point there."

"I've done it before. I've even been paid for escort services before—which, by the way, would help us fund the necessary provisions."

"Oh. Okay—in that case, you need a system from where merchants fly potentially endangered routes, eh?" Mo smiled, when she agreed with a nod. "Okay. Now, perhaps you should tell us where you want to go, so I can check whether I know any of the systems we might be passing."

CHAPTER THIRTY-TWO

Mo tapped a name on his panel. "Corfu. That's the place. It's a minor trans-shipment center at the edge of no man's land. Few merchants dare to go beyond, even with an escort. It's a kinda rough place, and I wouldn't think it wise to mention our guests there, but you'd get all kind of stuff there."

"And find all kinds of people, right?"

"True."

It was no place for a pretty woman like her, either, but the way she must have handled AP bullies and genetic experiments, she should be able to get by.

She confirmed his assumption by saying, "Don't worry. I know how to handle tough guys."

"Eight jumps, I'd guess," Yusef said and produced a sketched route. "Here—a wide arc around Hawthorne, and just a pass through Elton."

"Good solution," Mo said. "What does the computer say?"

"Oh—that one's bad. Four-sigma, and a major hazard to avoid. No, scratch that. Let me see—if we want to avoid that one, we'd have to pass here instead of Elton . . ."

Mo watched Syreen silently watch Yusef, as the pilot discarded one solution after the other.

Yusef wouldn't have done that before. Planning more than two jumps ahead, trying to find jumps that allow higher sigma levels, even considering untested routes — that's a lot of novelties. And fiddling with the fine controls for more than a centicycle, when would he have done that before?

100

"This," Yusef finally said. "I'll take more time to refine the later jumps, but I'm sure we can do six or seven sigma for all except the fourth. That's a fiver, and I don't see much room for improvement."

Syreen took her time to examine his solution.

"Excellent," she then said with a smile. "You're right, that's a five-sigma. If you want to avoid that, you could consider this detour instead."

Yusef squinted. "Two good sixers instead—I didn't see that."

"It's not obvious and not straightforward," Syreen admitted. "You'd not swap a good five-sigma for two six-sigma jumps ordinarily, as it'd take time and wear as well. But if you can achieve a double seven-sigma—and you'll see that'll work—it's worth a consideration. Okay—your initial solution for the next two was fine, so let's go."

"You don't want to refine them again?"

"After you did such a good job? No, I'll approve them."

Yusef seemed to grow several fingers taller.

All he'd needed all this time was a little motivation — a little more praise. That's the difference between a dull merchant's and a warship's board. And it's this young gal — around her, all kind of interesting things happen. We'll see how long we can appreciate this kind of interesting, and whether we'll soon long for some dullness.

Bumblebee did two more seven-sigma jumps in quick succession. Mo found himself becoming comfortable with this kind of travel.

"Unfold the sails," Syreen said to Yusef.

"Our capacitors are well charged," the pilot objected.

"Yes—and I want them almost full when we reach the next system. It's a pivot system that might be frequented. I don't want to be forced to stop there, and we have plenty of time now. Moreover, I think it's time to tell our passengers about our plans."

"If you think that helps," Mo said.

"Definitely. For one, uncertainty weakens people's morale and will to bear daily hardships, and for two, they deserve to know. Want to come along?"

"Sure."

"Okay. Yusef, you have the bridge."

"Yessir!" The pilot even imitated a salute.

Mo followed his commandant through the short corridor to the mess. He admired her matter-of-fact attitude, the way she moved, and yes, he also appreciated the view of her pretty ass.

Coincidence? She tossed him a smile over her shoulder and ambled on with swaying hips.

The door to the mess opened. When she stepped through, the chatter inside fell silent. Faces turned to her, and in those faces he could see the uncertainty she had mentioned.

"Call the others," she said. "I'll tell you all where we're going next and how I plan to keep you out of harm's way."

"When will we leave Gattaca?" Gwen asked.

"We already did," Syreen said. "Three jumps so far, along an unknown route. For now, we're safe. But please, be patient until we're all assembled. I don't want to say everything twice."

A girl with dark curls raised one hand. "Please—once you think we're really safe, well, uh—can we have a thank-you party?"

"Good idea. I'll consider that. What's your name?"

"Chiara."

"Chiara—I'll tell you once we've reached a place I consider safe, and you'll remind me of the party, okay?"

By and by, the women filed in. Some still wore AP standard suits, some had cut sleeves and legs off, some only wore shorts, a few of the last arrivals were nude. When she sensed no more latecomers, she raised a hand.

"Thank you for your attention. I want to tell you about our next steps. First, you may have missed the first three jumps we already made — we're no longer in the Gattaca system. The current star has no planets and isn't part of any frequented route, so we shouldn't expect any visitors here."

"Pirates?" June asked.

Syreen smiled. "I wouldn't advise any pirate approaching me while I'm in possession of a warship with working guns. Don't worry about pirates."

Mo stepped forward. "Have any of you heard the story of the *Light of Mandalay* and her pirate encounter?"

Some women nodded.

"For those who didn't, it's about a pirate, a merchant already boarded, and a tiny corvette — that's a warship, but about as big as two of your dorm rooms overall. The pirates threatened to kill their hostages. The corvette pilot wouldn't accept that blackmail, but instead shot the pirate's engine — only the engine — across a distance until then regarded impossible for even hitting an entire ship."

"I've heard that story," one woman said. "A nice fairytale to put your crew at ease. I wouldn't place my hope on such a knight in shining armor to appear."

Mo shook his head. "We're not talking about false hopes. I've heard that story, too, as told by the merchant captain, but I've met that captain before. I know he's real, and I know he doesn't tell fairytales. So I knew there had to be some truth in that story. I only couldn't tell how what he told should be possible, until I met our current captain, Syreen — and saw her perform more of those miracles. Like doing a seven-sigma jump. Those of you who traveled before, and not in the fridge, may have noticed you haven't noticed our jumps. In any case, the one you called a *knight in shining armor,* the one who shot that pirate, is our dear commandant herself."

"I'll try to believe that," Jona said. "As much as I still try to believe anyone could be foolish enough to descend to Gattaca's surface only to save a few forlorn harlots. However, the latter's a fact."

"I'm the one," Syreen said. "I'm the one, and once we've reached our destination, I'll show you my corvette *Raydancer*. Now, I want to talk with you about our next stop, though. It's called Corfu, and it's a bad place. You wouldn't want to be stranded there — worst of all, you wouldn't want to be found by the AP alive. Mo, would you give them some more insight?"

CHAPTER THIRTY-THREE

For a few steps, Syreen tried to negotiate around the stains on the floor before she gave up her futile attempt. Corfu Orbital was a mess, full stop. *Dirtside* had arrived here.

From the end of her docking bay corridor, three men were expectantly watching her approach. In their minds she could read lust paired with caution. She was already glad she had listened to Mo's advice and brought two guns along. She didn't plan to use them, but they most certainly shattered any impression of easy prey.

Her uniform added to the no-nonsense appearance. She hadn't been able to do much about the color, so she wore AP dress whites, but *Bumblebee's* equipment together with Martha's tailoring skills at least had helped with the stripes of a Fleet Commander in Charge plus several rows of stars — one for each successful kill.

All this glamour was probably lost on the men ahead. One tried to maintain an aura of authority, backed up by the two musclemen.

Accordingly, she ignored them and focused on the clerk. She stopped two steps before him and saluted. "Fleet Commander Syreen of Duchy frigate *Bumblebee.*"

He didn't meet her gaze. "*Bumblebee* is recorded as an AP ship."

"Possession has changed recently."

"How unusual."

"Unusual things happen in war."

Now he raised an eyebrow. "War. You're bringing war to

105

Corfu?"

"No. I'm offering escort services. I couldn't fail to notice quite a number of merchant ships following your station's orbit. Maybe some of them would grab the opportunity of traveling under my protection."

"Maybe. Should I have heard your name before?"

Now came the part she'd preferred to avoid—but she couldn't keep herself incognito and enter contracts with the guild or tap her accounts at the same time.

"Syreen. Registered with the guild as star angel."

Three heads jerked up, three sets of eyes focused on her.

"Star angels are just old lore," the clerk finally said.

"Check the guild roll."

He shook his head, but checked anyway. Again, his head jerked up, his eyes widened with surprise. "Syreen, registered as star angel. *Twice?*"

"It could become a habit."

"I . . . I didn't know—uh, well . . ."

"May I proceed?"

"Uh—oh—well, enjoy your stay on Corfu Orbital." He stepped aside and let her pass.

Only when she had reached the next junction did she hear him mumble, "Crap. I forgot to mention the harbor fees."

Syreen smiled to herself. *In exchange, I didn't ask for directions.*

The largest accumulation of mental noise had to be the food and entertainment area, Syreen guessed, and she was proven right. She glanced down the hallway and turned the opposite direction, where she expected and found shops and offices.

Walking down the corridor, she sensed left and right. At the far end, she finally found what she almost hadn't dared to hope for—a trader whose mind radiated less greed than the others and at least a hint of honor and sincerity. She entered

106

the shop. A lean man with short white hair rose from behind his desk.

"Welcome, Sir — uh, Madam. How can Akbay Goods be of service to you?"

"You are Mr. Akbay?"

"Just Akbay. That's my first name, if you like, uh — Admiral?"

"Fleet Commander Syreen."

"Fleet commander. That's more than commander?"

"That's more than admiral. It's the highest rank in our navy."

Akbay smiled. "I feel honored. Why did you pick my shabby shop?"

"I'm looking for an honest tradesman. I've never been to Corfu before, but my feelings say you're the one."

His smile became warmer. "Your feelings didn't betray you, Fleet Commander."

"Call me Syreen, Akbay."

"Syreen. I'm feeling honored, young lady. May I say, I've never seen a female skipper on Corfu before. It's a strange sight — a fleet commander running a merchant ship."

"I'm not running a merchant. I'm running a frigate."

"A warship — why do you bother to come here?"

"I'm offering escort services, protection against pirates."

"Oh. That's a hard job."

"Dangerous?"

"Oh, sure. No — it's hard to gain the trust of other merchants. They won't trust easily — the next skipper could be a competitor or a pirate."

"Pirates don't command frigates."

Akbay laughed. "You got a point there. But you don't need to convince me, you need to convince those skippers."

"I'll take care of that, don't worry."

"Oh, I'm not worried. I'm just trying to help the most

charming client I ever had and probably will ever have."

"I see—I've found a most charming trader."

He laughed again. "You're alright, Syreen. Now—what can I do for you?"

"It's dangerous out there, and it's even worse when you're going out with a less than amply stocked ship. I'd like to procure some provisions—better than AP emergency rations, for the occasional party too, but not too extravagant. I'm sure you've got just what I need."

CHAPTER THIRTY-FOUR

Returning to the station's noisiest place, Syreen kept her senses at full alert. She hadn't forgotten Mo's warning about Corfu being a rough place, and she knew where to expect ruffians.

Even her own home station had suffered its share of them, around the bars—until they'd all been blown to dust.

The memory still hurts, after all this time.

She sighed.

I won't forget. This crime must not remain without consequences, if only to discourage potential imitators. Perhaps I'm already too late to save my own people, but I still can save others.

There was a slight rush of air.

Who's sneaking up on me?

That cutter could hurt, too.

She turned toward the young man who'd just approached her with his dangerous tool. "Hi, cutie. Know a quieter place for us?"

He knew, and a few centicycles later, she felt refreshed and ready for some serious bargaining. Her victim would eventually overcome his sudden weakness, but not before she had departed.

Where do I start?

Five venues in a row, each with its share of filth, noise and inebriated patrons—each skipper a prospect, each man a potential harassment.

Each doorway held a bouncer, and they all watched her

109

approach. When she reached the closest man, he frowned.

"No hookers inside."

She placed both hands on her gun handles. "Who do you call a hooker, son?"

He shrank back. "Hey, you can't bring guns to the station!"

"I already did, son."

"But . . ." He shook his head. "No one has guns."

"Fleet officers do have guns."

"Fleet? What fleet?"

"Duchy Fleet."

"Never heard of a douche-y fleet." Now he smiled. "What are you shipping? What trade?"

"I'm shipping big guns. I'm in the escort business, shooting pirates and such. Anything you need a frigate for."

"A *frigate?*"

"Yep. A warship, a pilot, all you need to get a school of haulers safely through. I expect to find some clients here."

"Oh."

"May I pass now?"

"Uh — sure."

He stepped aside, still eyeing her guns.

She entered the venue.

Right behind the door, Syreen stopped again. The place was anything but well-lit or well-vented. The patrons were anything but well-groomed, sober, or happy.

That she could approach the counter unmolested was partially owing to her guns, partially to her mental command.

"Hey, gal, how did you pass our bouncer?" asked the bartender.

"By showing him my guns. I'm commanding the frigate *Bumblebee,* and I'm not someone to mess with. The next round is on me, if I may make an announcement."

"Oh, well, have a try." He smiled and gestured at the

chattering crowd.

It wouldn't be easy to get their attention, unless one could cheat. Syreen did exactly that.

Listen. You're curious — what's a chick in uniform doing here?

Merchant captains and crews, already idling in the same spot for a while, were curious by default — her little mental nudge fell on fertile ground. By and by, they noticed her presence and ceased talking.

"Skippers, listen." She climbed a chair. "I'm Syreen. I'm commanding the frigate *Bumblebee,* and I'm offering escort service. Should any of you have heard about an impossible shot that saved the *Light of Mandalay* — I'm the one who did it."

That statement caused a number of remarks, but soon, the people were ready to listen again.

"I'll accept proposals for the next route. Wherever you have to go, I'll get you there, jump by jump. Maybe you won't do the shortest route, but together with your fellow ships, you'll be safe."

"What's that impossible shot talk?" one man asked.

Syreen spoke up first. "It was a pirate, already docked to a merchant. He was asking me to surrender. I was commanding a corvette — somewhat smaller than a frigate, you know. The pirate captain tried to blackmail me, you can imagine how. My answer was three shots — at the power plant, at the bridge, at the aft hyperdrive section. Each was a precise hit, even across fifty light seconds."

"I've heard such a story," one man said. "Much exaggerated, I thought. But you claim you were there?"

"I'm the one, the one Captain Kasai called a *star angel.* You don't have to believe all that, but my frigate is a fact you can check with your own eyes."

"What's your price?"

She smiled. "Depends on the sum quoted on your export declaration. Or I could ask for a flat charge."

"How much?"

Syreen had previously asked Mo. Merchants running remote and dangerous routes like these weren't rich. She had traveled on such ships—skippers could hardly afford even the most urgent repairs, much less the charges for a decent escort.

Still, they were carrying valuable goods—and they were pressed to deliver them eventually, otherwise docking fees and the cost of living would eat away their little savings.

Syreen had also checked the star maps. Navigating this part of the galaxy wasn't trivial, but for her, it was no challenge.

"I must earn my docking fees," she continued to her audience. "I can't ask for less than five-hundred thousand credits per stop, no matter how many jumps we need, no matter how many of you are coming along."

She could see and sense their disappointment. Even if they divided her charges among them, such a sum had to come from somewhere.

"Payable one tencycle after safe arrival at the agreed destination. I will do the jump calculations for the entire convoy, and I guarantee five-sigma or better for every jump. I won't promise six-sigma for all jumps, but by traveling with me you will definitely save on your maintenance costs."

There were excited whispers among the merchants. Every credit not spent on maintenance was available for protection.

"You said, payable after safe arrival? You don't ask for an advance?"

"Correct. Once I deliver you to your destination, you have one tencycle to negotiate an advance by your customers there and pay me. After that, it's up to you whether you'll tag along to the next stop or go your own way—however, you'd have to discuss that with your fellows."

"Will you offer us a safe return with the same conditions?"

"Not exactly a return. I'm taking you along traveling toward my own destination, but yes, you can follow me there."

"What's that destination?"

"Woo."

"That's across the entire sector—right through the wild zone."

"Correct. I don't fear the wild zone." She spread her arms. "Discuss my conditions and your options with your fellow skippers. I'll do my round through the other venues, and when I'm done there, you can contact me aboard my ship. If you're interested, we can set up a route that suits all of you, I'm sure."

CHAPTER THIRTY-FIVE

Syreen hadn't expected Mo to welcome her back aboard, but his curiosity shone like a beacon.

"I'm relieved you're back safely," he said. "Any trouble?"

She remembered her encounter with the cutter. "Not at all. Piece of cake. Nice people—at least if you're carrying guns."

He grinned. "So my advice was helpful?"

"Quite so, thank you. We should have at least ten prospects in the morning, perhaps twelve."

"So many? Did you quote below what I told you?"

"Just the opposite—I told them I'd charge five-hundred thousand per stop, no matter how many jumps."

"Five? No one can afford that."

"Payable one tencycle after arrival—if they can negotiate an advance on their sales, they can afford me."

"And be stuck with a broken ship."

"Again, just the opposite. I offered to do their jump calculations—actually, I'll have to insist on that, so that we don't run into each other upon reentry, and I don't want to have my flock spread over the entire system, in case we run into pirates. I promised them all jumps to be five-sigma or better. In fact, I'm sure I can do at least six."

Mo considered that, then nodded. "Indeed. That makes the deal look attractive."

"Did our provisions arrive already?"

"Yes. There was a guy—Akbay's the name—with a huge load. Haiki and Yusef had a hard time finding a place for all that stuff. I told them, they'd be glad to have it once we're

114

traveling on. I guess some merchants will call up destinations near the wild zone."

"Sure. Some will come through with us."

"Through?"

"Yes. I need to cross over to Woo, and I don't want to return deep into the AP—a pirate zone is way less dangerous for me right now."

"Before Gattaca, I'd have called you crazy. Now I know better, but I still think that's a bad idea."

She grinned. "I know. I hope the AP thinks the same."

The merchant shook his head. "This will come to a bad end."

"We'll see. I'll take a nap now."

Two cycles later, Syreen woke up again. She felt refreshed, her beast soothed, and after a cold navy-style shower, she was ready to face whatever monsters this galaxy had in store for her.

On the corridor, she met Jona. Her nude body was in good shape, she smelled fresh, and radiated some kind of excitement.

"I've been waiting for you," the woman announced.

Syreen smiled. "What kind of ambush is this?"

"Just an offer. You might want to stay away from the blokes—for respect, discipline, and everything. If you feel lonely—well, I know how to please another woman. You can call me anytime."

"Oh, that's nice of you." She felt a tingle between her legs. "Indeed, a good idea. Why don't we say it's *anytime* now?"

"Now?" Jona needed a moment, then she grinned. "Sure, why not?"

Because I'd rather ride a big cock. Out of the question now. So, let's check the other side today. There's still so much to learn.

She could feel her beast stirring. *Curious, too? Be patient.*

Jona was right behind her when she entered her cabin

115

again. She could feel the other woman's breath on her neck, while Jona's hands started exploring her. A brief and gentle touch to the side of her breast, a brush through her hair, then she felt wet lips at her earlobe, behind her ears, and at her neck.

Syreen closed her eyes and imagined a man playing with her. A man with a prominent chest and little equipment below, but with these skilled hands running up and down her sides, such a deficit no longer mattered.

She lost her senses for time. Someone played a tune on her body, matching a different, distant melody she hadn't noticed before.

How and when did I lose my uniform? Ah!

Her thighs were already wet, from her own sweat and lubrication as well as that insatiable tongue that now explored the depths between her inner labia.

With wide-spread legs, her back against the bulkhead, she could only enjoy, could only moan, not talk.

More!

Jona obeyed. Her tongue now circled Syreen's clitoris, while her fingers explored the slippery and dark depths.

More!

There was room enough for Jona's hand, slowly moving back and forth.

More!

The pushing fist helped Syreen imagine *Assiduous'* large primary plug.

More!

A finger found its way into her anus.

Yes! Come!

She came with a long moan, echoed by Jona's lustful cry — and another distant cheer.

The finger in her rear disappeared first, then the fist slowly relaxed and left, followed by a gush of her juice.

"Oh!" Jona sank back on the floor.

Syreen let herself slide down the bulkhead and landed in a puddle. She didn't care. Instead, she reached forward and placed a hand on the trembling woman's shoulder. "You're okay?"

Jona looked up. "I came!" A tear ran down her cheek. "I . . . I came!"

"I came, too," Syreen said quietly. "You didn't promise too much. Thank you, Jona."

"But I—I've never felt such lust before. How can that be?"

"Hush, don't ask. Enjoy."

"But—"

"No *but* today. It's my turn now."

Syreen let her fingers run down from shoulder to breast, to hip, across the firm buttock. "Relax. Let it happen. Let me try what you taught me."

Enjoy.

CHAPTER THIRTY-SIX

Syreen silently left her cabin, watched the door close between her and the now sleeping Jona. After their third, joint climax, the young woman hadn't been able to bear any more.

Syreen could feel Mo's tension growing, so she went straight to the bridge.

"Hi, Mo. Any calls yet?"

"Fifteen so far."

"You expect more to follow?"

"Not really. As there are only fifteen merchants in this system with us . . ."

"What are they saying?"

"They all want to go. To Harmony, Quito, Pompeii, Backwater—"

"Such a place exists?"

"You'd be amazed if you checked the library for names."

"Another time. What else is on the list?"

"Nizwa, Kathmandu, Chengdu, Puerto La Cruz, Santana, Kumasi, Zamora, Le Mans. That's it."

"Twelve destinations, fifteen ships?"

"Yes—we have three groups of two. For Harmony, Quito, and Zamora. They suggest we should go there first, as they're paying two shares—six shares together for the round trip."

"I already told them there'll be no round trip. We won't return here."

"Oh, sure, but they'll probably risk a solo return along a route that's been cleared by you. From Zamora, it's only two jumps to the Corfu-Harmony route."

"You already checked for a solution?"

"Several." Mo smiled and waved a hand. "Hey, I'm not just a passenger. If I can't do much else, I can at least play with the library—anyway, there's basically no straightforward solution to visit all of them. You'd have to zigzag, which means a lot of extra jumps for most of the ships."

"Yes. I don't know much about logistics, but as far as I know, merchants don't just deliver goods, they also pick up some—if such a remote planet has anything useful to offer."

"That's the case. Otherwise it wouldn't pay to go there—they couldn't afford imports. However, most of their stuff isn't worth much on the central planets. It's exotics, rare earths, gems, sometimes drugs, mostly small amounts."

"I'd assume one or two of them would be short on things others could offer."

"Yes, but it's not worth shipping them unless someone sails that route anyway . . ." Mo stopped. "Oh, yes, I understand what you're proposing. You could even make a small profit—tailored to what they can afford. Gal, there's a good merchant lost in you."

"While we pretend I haven't made my decision yet, would you ask around? Asking for provisioning options should be legitimate."

"Playing your purser? I can do that, and give them an idea I might do a little side business."

"Do that. Meanwhile I'll check the obvious and less obvious jumps around these systems."

"You don't want to go out shooting pirates?"

"I won't hesitate to shoot every pirate I meet, but with a merchant fleet in our wake, I'll rather play safe. This is not the time for a crusade against piracy."

"I'm glad to hear that. Even a frigate isn't invulnerable, you know?"

"I know. I've shot bigger ones with smaller ones, remember?"

CHAPTER THIRTY-SEVEN

After a few calls, Mo not only had a first idea of a profitable route but also the feeling that his questions had triggered similar ideas with the other merchants, too.

Good. If they buy that idea, to make the most of this impossible trip, they'll more likely accept Syreen's plans for the route.

Here came a return call.

"*Bumblebee,* this is *Shiny Tin Can.* Simon Hopper speaking."

"Hi. *Bumblebee* here. I'm Mo."

"Mo? I'd like to talk to your captain about our route."

"She's not on the bridge, Simon."

"Well—I'm curious. I've never heard of a warbird skipper making profitable proposals. What's going on here?"

"Simon, she's considerate. She cares. That's going on here."

"Such a thing as a considerate warbird skipper exists? You're pulling my leg." Captain Hopper didn't wait for Mo's response. "I've done a little research about that star angel story she told us. There seems to be some truth behind it—the entry in the rolls exists. Twice, and I've never heard of a star angel registered twice. Not that I'd ever met one. Are you authorized to give me some more background?"

"I'm not exactly authorized, but I can give you a summary. She's Fleet Commander in Charge of Duchy Fleet. You'll find the Duchy in your star catalog, and when you check for the route to Kyris, you'll see how it matches her story."

"Duchy Fleet, huh? *Bumblebee* is recorded as an AP frigate."

"Yes. The records need to be updated."

"You're saying she's running a stolen ship?"

120

"Not stolen. Captured. Won in war, in one piece, no casualties. She knows her business."

"At least *you* say so."

"I say so, yes. I decided to entrust my life to the first star angel in generations—the first double star angel ever. What I've experienced so far has exceeded my wildest expectations."

"You're her crew, so you're biased."

Mo considered telling the merchant how he became her crew, but discarded that option. "Naturally. But you asked for background."

"Indeed. Well, thank you for giving me some insight. I will follow your advice and check my catalog for more details. Please tell your captain about my request regarding our route."

"Sure. Bye."

Mo disconnected and smiled. Captain Hopper had already bought into the deal, he just wasn't ready to consciously accept it yet.

There had to be some real danger on their route. There was no other explanation for such a large number of merchants to stay in place. They had been waiting, most likely for one of their own bold enough to sail on, or for running out of money and being forced to leave.

With a frigate as their protection, there was no option but to go. Indeed, the only open question was their route, and if Syreen, Yusef and Mo could come up with a reasonable proposal, they'd accept it—after more or less complaining and bickering.

Which brings back the question of how such a reasonable proposal could look. Let's see—nobody out there seems to need stuff from Le Mans.

Mo's skipper—*pardon, fleet commander*—entered the bridge with the usual grace, but a hint of unrest in her face.

"Ready to go?" she asked.

He shook his head. "The merchants proposed twelve different routes. There's just one thing in common—most skippers would go to Harmony first. It's the closest destination, only three jumps from Corfu, and it's on the way to most other destinations, perhaps except for Zamora."

"Harmony first? Okay, and from there?"

"Some prefer Quito, but Kumasi would be just a little detour, and they have stuff that Quito could need."

"Harmony, Kumasi, Quito. Yes, that's quite an obvious solution." She called up a map. "Only we miss Backwater that way. However, if we make a circle from Harmony through Santana and Backwater, we need only one extra jump to Kumasi. Let me show you . . ."

I shouldn't be surprised.

Still, it was amazing to see her adding and optimizing routes with a few flicks of her fingers while arranging their stops. It wasn't just drafting—he could see the sigma levels of her unrefined solutions, and none of the ten jumps were below six.

A Navigator with capital N, indeed.

"From there, we could reach Zamora in three jumps, but it's an easy four-jump route via Pompeii. This is the start of a twisted S-curve that would continue through Chengdu, Nizwa, Puerto La Cruz, Le Mans, and Kathmandu to Woo. Thirty-four jumps overall, and the worst part is the four-jump leg from Chengdu to Nizwa with two five-sigmas, but with a chance to re-provision here—Second Stop."

"What?"

Syreen shrank back from his shout.

"Sorry," he said, calmer again. "Second Stop is the name of a legendary pirate hub. I didn't even know it was mapped." *And its location explains why the others are so nervous. This is a dangerous region indeed.*

"Access to that data was marked as restricted. It's a

military library."

"So I shouldn't have seen this?"

She grinned. "Duchy policy—as defined by the current Fleet Commander in Charge—is to keep the crew aware of all important intel."

Mo nodded.

With a stern face, she continued, "A pirate hub. What does that mean? Lots of vessels with guns?"

"Hardly. They can't earn their next forwine by idling around a station. Perhaps one or two, but the station will be armed. It's probably not a wise move to go there."

"Let me see—we could give the merchants a little rest and have a look at Second Stop. They could arrive a tencycle or two later, after we've cleared the area."

"You can't just go in there and clear anything. It's an independent system."

"According to this data, they've joined the guild. They're supposed to cooperate with us against piracy. Should they actively support pirates, though, they'd be treated as such. Or, they might have issued a letter of marque, in which case we're talking about war."

"A letter of what?"

"A document entitling the bearer to capture other ships by violent means."

"Ah, okay—what do you mean, talking about war?"

"If any independent nation sends out ships to capture civil traders, that's an act of war against which every involved nation may take appropriate action. Should they shoot or even only threaten to shoot a trader escorted by us, we'd be involved. I'd like that."

"But they'd have to shoot first. Which means someone might be hurt."

"Their wisest move would be shooting me first. Which means our merchants are safe."

"Until they've finished us."

"Won't happen."

There was an unvoiced *trust me* lingering in the air, but he wasn't yet ready to trust her that far.

"Are you willing to take that risk? What about your mission?"

"Yes. That's something I'll consider. As discussed before, I don't want to take unnecessary risks. Now, leaving Second Stop aside, what do you think about our route from the merchant point of view?"

"Our paired clients will complain about the tail, that's for sure. They'd prefer returning to Corfu. Other than that, it's the best we can offer, and it offers some business options, too."

"Thank you. Would there be better business options if we exchanged some destinations?"

"Yes and no. Yes, there would be options on the reverse route, perhaps even more profitable, and no, they wouldn't be worth the extra time and jumps. Without the pirate threat, there would be a lot of traffic, though—and with an established six-sigma route, trade would soar."

"Okay. So we've got an offer?"

"You're the skipper. Oh—I wouldn't mention Second Stop."

She returned his warm smile. "Of course not."

CHAPTER THIRTY-EIGHT

Syreen terminated the call and shook her head. "Not again."
Yusef looked up. "Still bickering?"

"Yes. They can't accept a no."

"They're merchants. That's what merchants do — negotiating."

"And I'm a navigator and commandant. Computers and people do as I order. That doesn't match."

"I think you're doing fine."

"Thanks. I won't change the route anyway. Come along or stay behind, that's the choice. Maybe some of them will leave us early."

"And fly solo?"

"There's that return route from Zamora. The impatient ones might dare to go."

"Right into the pirates' jaws. They'll have their spies on Corfu, and by now, everyone knows where to lie in wait for some fat haulers without escort."

"In vain." She smiled. "How far did you get with your calculations?"

"I have two options for each jump, convoy style, as you said, plus an emergency breakup sequence, also for each jump, and I've done two rounds of refinements each. The second refinement yielded little improvement, so I decided to do a last fine tuning when we're there."

"Perfect. Yusef, you make me proud."

"I had a good teacher."

"You didn't need a teacher. You needed motivation. The

125

navigating was there all the time."

"I'll never reach your skill level, though."

"No. That's a fact—you can't hear the stars' songs. But aside from that, you're the best pilot I've traveled with until now. None of the others soaked it all up that fast. Now, why don't you prepare another return option from Zamora to Corfu? A new route pirates won't expect?"

Yusef looked up in surprise, and then grinned. "Nice idea. But do you think our merchants would try an unknown route without our guidance?"

"After they've done fourteen jumps you've prepared? What's your guess?"

"Oh. Yes, once they've seen what we do, they might accept my proposal."

"They surely will. And they'll make you offers."

Yusef briefly closed his eyes and took a deep breath. When he looked straight into her face again, she could feel his sincerity.

"I will stay with you, wherever you go. Now that I know what you can do, I want to see it all. This galaxy is due for a change, and I can have a seat in the front row. I won't throw that one-in-a-billion chance away."

His emotions almost overwhelmed her. There was so much more behind his words. Envy—but only for that part of her skills he'd never achieve. Fascination, curiosity, respect, admiration . . . and love.

PART THREE—EXPLORATION

CHAPTER THIRTY-NINE

"*Bumblebee,* Syreen speaking. Prepare for first jump in ten. Say goodbye to Corfu and look forward to a smooth journey."

You have no clue yet how smooth it will be. Your computers can't flag a seven-sigma jump, so it looks like a good six — until you've done it.

Yusef's calculations had already stirred some excitement. While merchants occasionally traveled in groups, they rarely ever jumped in a tight formation. That was something the military did.

Syreen had patiently explained her reasoning — the formation kept them close to their single escort, thus offering them the best protection possible. She simply couldn't stay with every ship if those were scattered across the next system, and getting them together for the next jump would cost precious time.

By agreeing to the formation and using Yusef's solution they'd save time, reduce wear, and improve their own protection. Three arguments not lost even to the most individualistic merchant.

By and by, fifteen ships acknowledged her call.

She checked their positions again. Some ships weren't perfectly aligned, but well within the allowance she had established for their journey, so that they wouldn't run into each other upon reentry.

"Jump in one," Yusef spoke to the internal com. "Get ready, girls."

Nothing to worry about. Ready or not, they'll hardly notice.

She sent a last goodbye to the central star and imagined receiving a sigh, then they were gone.

A new system, a new song, confirming the successful jump—Syreen could check for their convoy first, before their initial scan. That was how she was able to notice something fundamentally wrong, just in time.

She nudged her stick, made *Bumblebee* sway to a side, then let the ship flip around and fire two of its four forward guns.

"Whoah!" Yusef shouted. "What was that?"

Syreen already trained her bow at the next merchant, and shot again—this time only one gun, with less energy.

A flip of her fingers activated the radio. *"Veronica's Smile,* don't even dare to move anywhere without orders. I'm aiming at your bridge. Be sure I won't miss you, as I didn't miss the gun you'd been hiding in your cargo bay. To all—I had to eliminate gun and bridge of the *Athabasca* after their shot at my ship. That hauler is currently without steering, so stay clear. We will deal with survivors later."

While she was waiting for first reactions, she kept her attention directed at the second armed merchant—a pirate by definition, as merchant ships weren't allowed to carry guns.

"*Bumblebee, this is Captain Aziz of the* Carthago. *My readings confirm that* Athabasca *shot first, but they also show that you dodged the shot. My pilot says you'd have been hit if you hadn't moved. How did you know?"*

"Captain Aziz, I didn't know until he started turning his ship. When he released the shot, I dodged."

"That's what it looked like, but—no one can dodge a pulse shot."

"Captain Aziz, I can, and I did it before. My senses work faster than light."

"That's nonsense. No one can sense faster than light."

"Your readings contain evidence. Check the timing again and calculate it back—my maneuver started when the shot was released. There is no other explanation. Had the shot been staged, I still couldn't have done such a tight synchronization."

There was a brief pause. *"My pilot says the numbers match your claim."*

Another call joined in. *"Captain Hopper, of* Shiny Tin Can. *My data backs her claim, too, and I have no clue how she could do it. Moreover, did anyone else notice that our jump was way too smooth even for a six-sigma calculation? My pilot says, it was better by a full level, seven-sigma, if such existed."*

Several other captains confirmed his observation. Finally, Hopper addressed her again. "Bumblebee, *can you explain?"*

"It was a seven-sigma jump solution, planned as such and executed to the point. I didn't tell you before because you wouldn't have believed me, but I promised you five-sigma or better, and I plan to maintain this quality level. In fact, most of our jumps will be seven-sigma, but we might have to do one fiver or two and a few sixers."

Hopefully that'll make them forget the other topic. Anyway, there's work to do.

She muted her line.

"Yusef, can you operate the gun controls?"

"Uh — dunno, what do you need?"

"I need you to shoot *Veronica's Smile's* engines in case she tries to run while I'm taking our shuttle to pay them a visit." She noticed an incoming call. "Wait — Yes? Syreen speaking."

"Ruben, of Santiago. *I've talked with Karim — together, we could take care of* Athabasca *survivors. We have sidearms, and we'd offer to have a look while you're probably dealing with* Veronica. *We assume any survivors will be glad to be picked up, instead of staying on that wreck, so there won't be much resistance. I assume skipper, pilot and gunner are gone anyway."*

"Sounds like a valid assumption. Okay, Ruben, thank you for the offer. Proceed as proposed, but proceed with caution."

"Sure. Thank you for saving our asses today."

And your assets, too. "You're welcome. That's what you hired me for."

She turned to Yusef again. "You think you can do that?"

"Sure. Seems quite straightforward—I see you already locked one gun on the target."

"I did. Otherwise, use your own good judgment."

She switched to the internal line. "Mo, could you assist Yusef on the bridge? Thanks. Haiki, can we meet at the shuttle bay?"

A moment later, Mo appeared in the door. "What can I do?"

"Yusef is taking the gun. Can you keep an eye on the long-range scans and answer the radio? I must hop over and clean a pirate ship."

"Sure. You're taking Haiki along?"

"Yes. He will watch the shuttle while I'm going in."

"Okay. Good luck."

Luck is no legit element of planning. Who said that? My flight trainer, and he said it's in the Books.

CHAPTER FORTY

With caution, Syreen directed *Bumblebee's* small assault shuttle toward *Veronica's Smile's* airlock.

"Did you really dodge a pulse shot?" Haiki asked.

"Yes."

"How could you do that?"

"I just felt it coming."

"Is that some kind of premonition?"

"Uh—yes, kind of. I'm aware of things that happen around me the very moment they happen—and the speed of light doesn't limit this kind of awareness."

"Sounds like magic."

"Yes—like hyperjumps. They're faster than light, too."

Haiki laughed. "Sometimes, Mo says I'm doing magic, too—when I fix something with wires and patches and it works better than the factory solution. But what you're doing—that's something different."

"I'm not doing anything. I'm just listening."

"Don't get me wrong. I'm glad you're listening. What does that ship ahead sing to you?"

His wording made her smile. *He's listening, too.*

"Malice, fear, and determination. They're not beaten yet."

"What could they possibly do now? Yusef is watching our back."

"Oh—that's easy. They might have kept the original crew hostage, and by threatening to hurt them they'll try making me surrender our shuttle to them. Next, they'll try the same on Yusef—shoot, and you kill your own skipper. If that would work, they'd gain access to a frigate. But rest assured, I won't let that happen."

"More magic?"

"This time, I'll try my silk tongue."

Syreen grinned, and he grinned back.

"Almost there." She gave their shuttle another nudge, then activated the magnets. "Connected. Keep an eye on the readings and be prepared for an emergency launch—in case they blow up the ship."

"Oh—okay. Sure, I'll be ready to go." He pointed at her uniform. "No evac suit?"

"No. I don't want to appear overly cautious. You can take one, if you prefer."

"Oh—never mind."

The inner airlock door, made from strong and solid steel, seemed too thin to contain all those evil feelings she could sense beyond. Syreen wasn't particularly eager to meet the originators of such emotions, but that was what she had come for . . . and her beast looked forward to that encounter. So . . .

Let's have some fun together.

She pushed the opener button. The door swung aside and unveiled a scene of appropriate—and expected—nastiness.

Two men were on their knees, tied and gagged. One was standing behind them, a tightly pressed switch in one hand, a needle gun in the other.

"The other two are on the bridge, and my mate will treat them bad if you don't do as asked. First, put your guns down."

"I didn't bring any guns." She smiled, spread her arms and made a full turn. *You're curious. Keep that switch squeezed and put the gun away. Tell your mate about that unarmed hot chick you're facing.*

"Stay where you are. I want to see your hands all the time."

Syreen nodded and spread her arms.

The pirate stuffed the gun into the hip holster. "No tricks. I'm still holding the trigger."

She nodded again.

"Doug, she's here. Alone and unarmed. What do you make of that?"

"Ask her."

"Okay. Girl, what's your plan? Where's the trick?"

"No trick. I have to convince you to surrender to me, whatever it takes."

Now he started to grin. "Whatever it takes?"

"Yes."

"What if I asked you to undress?"

"Ask and find out."

"Okay. Undress."

Syreen smiled. Her uniform jacket went down first, then she opened her blouse. Mental control wasn't required to stir his interest. His glance seemed to be glued to her bared chest.

Yuck – what a slime pit his mind is.

"Doug, you should see these cute tits."

"What – she did?"

"She's just pulling down her pants. Hey – no undies! Oh my, Doug, she's hot."

"Stay where you are, Pete. I'm coming down. We can take turns with trigger and gun."

"You better hurry." Pete was fumbling with the switch. The growing bulge in his pants indicated an emergency.

Lock it and put it away. You need free hands to unzip your pants.

She stepped out of her pants and placed her feet wide.

Wide – were his eyes, too.

"Do you see something you want?" she teased him.

For a moment, that statement seemed to trigger suspicions. She intervened. *What you see is what you asked for.*

Another man arrived.

That must be Doug. Time to end this game.

Directed at them, she ordered, *Face down on the floor. Both of*

134

you.

Both men dropped down as if shot.

Don't move.

First Syreen gathered their triggers and guns and put them aside. Then she removed the explosive charges from the merchants' clothes, unfastened their ties, and removed both their gags.

"You're safe. Now go and take care of your mates on the bridge."

To her amazement, only one of them climbed to his feet, briefly struggled for balance, and left.

The other rose, too, but only to pick up her clothes and hold the jacket out to her. "Ma'am."

She accepted the jacket and slipped into the sleeves. Her pants followed, then her boots. The merchant patiently watched and waited until she stood straight again.

"I don't know how you did it," he said.

"Military secret. I'm Syreen, Duchy Fleet. When did they take over? Before or after Corfu?"

"Long before Corfu. We've been locked away for hectocycles. I wasn't aware we had already arrived there. I'm Terry Palmer, and I'd been the captain of this ship until they seized it. That was on our trip from Hobart to Takahashi."

"Okay, Captain Palmer. I'm curious about your whole story, but we should fly on to Harmony first. I don't want to linger in this uninhabited system any longer than I have to. Sorry I had to shoot one of your freight compartments when I took out the gun."

"More military secrets? I didn't notice a jump away from Corfu, I didn't notice any severe damage to my ship—who are you?"

"Once we're on our way, the other merchants can fill you in. For now, you need to know you're part of a convoy of fifteen haulers and one frigate—mine—on your way to Harmony and eventually to Quito, where your ship supposedly had been bound."

"That's true."

"Okay. We negotiated a fixed fee with the other merchants. As you had no say in that, I won't ask anything from you until Harmony. From there on, it's your call."

"That's most generous of you—for me, you're like an angel."

"Spot on. I'm a registered star angel."

He stared at her. "You're the one who saved the *Light of Mandalay?*"

"Yes."

"By all gods in the sky." He dropped to his knees, covered his face in his hands, and wept.

A wave of relief washed over her and almost made her stumble.

Syreen lost control, but only for a moment. The two pirates recognized an opportunity. They jumped up and dashed for their guns. The only potential witness was still burying his eyes in his hands—*remain so.*

Now.

Her beast needed no other instructions. One jump from standing took her past the merchant and between pirates and guns. Disbelief and horror mixed up nicely in their minds and their faces. The latter won when she showed her canines.

Their fear tasted so sweet, but even sweeter was their realization they'd now pay for all the wrong they'd done—that there could be no mercy, only pain, and death in the end.

Revenge wasn't Syreen's goal. The pirates had to pay, had to provide compensation for the power she'd invested. Yet she could taste their pain when she drained them of almost all of their blood.

Almost. *There are still some questions unanswered. I want to know it all. Until then, you're not allowed to die. Not by my hand, nor by your own.*

When she left them alone, she beamed with power.

Time to get away from here.

"Rise, Captain Palmer. Your mates on the bridge need you."

The merchant looked up. "Who—what are you?"

"I'm a *Navigator*."

He shook his head. "What's a *navigator?*"

"I sense hyperspace, I hear the stars sing—I make sailing the skies safer. I protect those entrusted to my care. That's a Navigator." *And I command a living ship. You needn't know that yet.*

She glanced at the pirates. "Come."

CHAPTER FORTY-ONE

Mo watched his captain enter the bridge with her usual grace. She took her seat, tapped her panel, and said, "Yusef, I'm active. Thank you."

"Any trouble?" Mo asked.

"No. I was able to convince the pirates to give up and follow me. Haiki locked them away. I'll interrogate them once we've arrived at Harmony. I don't want to linger here any longer. Do you know anything about the *Athabasca?*"

"Yes. Ruben of the *Santiago* called. They've picked up four crew members. The ship's severely damaged. Ruben proposed sending it sunward, so that it can't become a traffic hazard."

"What do you think?"

"Skippers sailing this region aren't rich. Losing their ship is like cutting the lifeline."

"What could they do? Work on a different ship?"

"Well—I wouldn't hire anyone here. Who knows—might be a pirate, cutting your throat while you're asleep. Not worth taking the risk unless you absolutely have to. No, they're most likely stuck dirtside. Or they'll end up in the pirate business themselves, out of desperation. Not that I'd accept such an excuse, don't get me wrong."

"Okay. What do you think of the ship?"

"*Athabasca?* Well—I didn't see it myself. You shot it. What did you hit?"

"Bridge, and gun—inside a cargo bay."

"The cargo bay doesn't matter. Such things can be fixed.

The bridge is a different story. You can't control a ship without a bridge."

"Aren't there secondary controls in the engine department?"

"Oh, yes, every ship has them. Mostly for wharf maneuvers, so that engineers needn't run back and forth when relocating a hauler. But there's no library and all."

"They won't need a library right now. We're doing the jump calculations for them anyway. Call Ruben and ask the *Athabasca's* skipper if he wants to explore that option. Tell them I'd like to sail within a cycle, and if everything else works fine, there are only two more seven-sigma jumps to Harmony, where they can patch their holes and have some basic gear installed."

"They'll kiss your feet for a chance to keep their ship. I'll talk with Ruben."

"But you said you'd prefer to leave soon?" Yusef chimed in.

Syreen nodded. "I said so, yes. But if there's a chance to prevent desperate people becoming pirates, I have to take it. Until then, we have to watch out for new arrivals."

"You expect visitors?" Yusef asked.

"Indeed. Why else would you ambush the entire convoy here? They were eight people. They could never expect to capture thirteen others, so they probably had to call for reinforcements. They could expect to nail us down here, though, so we might have some time left. Meanwhile, I'd like to have a closer look at the secondary arrival point."

CHAPTER FORTY-TWO

Yusef couldn't make up his mind—should he hope for more pirates to appear before they left, or should he hope for the peaceful continuation of their already troubled journey?

He'd like to see his captain perform another miracle, but what if her lucky streak was over? Where luck was relative, he mused. Two ships were already damaged, one nearly crippled, and they had only done the first of more than forty jumps.

In exchange, Syreen had taught him how to calculate seven-sigma jumps—he'd only recently discovered and understood some of her modifications to the computer programming. She had dodged a pulse shot, had precisely eliminated the pirates on one ship and the gunners on another and had *convinced* two more pirates to surrender without a gun.

Yusef focused on his own tasks again. The other pilots had quickly accepted his new two-jump solution, both seven-sigma, and within a quartercycle, they'd arrive at Harmony.

He looked over his shoulder, right into her smile.

"No worries, Yusef."

"I'm not worried when you're here."

"Most charming. Get us ready for jump, now."

"Yessir. This is *Bumblebee*, Yusef speaking. Prepare for jump in ten and acknowledge." He switched. "Crew and guests, prepare for smooth jump in nine."

Back to routine. Long-range scan—unchanged. Engines and emitters—fine. Secondary aggregates—oh. "Haiki, can you have a look at the converter readings, please?"

"Already on it, Yusef. I had to fiddle with the settings. Ninety percent ladies, that's not within the standard parameters."

"Any trouble?"

Haiki shook his head. "No—just a question of individual settings, as I said. We're fine."

Jump in four. Yusef checked the scans again. Syreen would want perfect results, so—

"*Veronica's Smile*, you're pitching upward by zero point two. Please trim to convoy trajectory."

"What? Oops, confirmed, *Bumblebee*. We trim."

This time, he didn't have to turn around. He could sense her smile—she was pleased.

It's fun to do a better job if it's appreciated.

His board told him nothing new about the jump.

I'm getting a feel for this. Well, at least I'm able to notice such jumps, and that my ship is doing fine. Now, scans.

The merchants were doing fine, too. They dropped out of the hyperplane in almost the same formation they had entered it, perfectly aligned, only *Veronica's Smile* sailed a bit lower than planned.

The long-range scans unveiled no surprises. No other ships, no obstacles, no deviation from the planned route.

"This is *Bumblebee*, Yusef speaking. You already have your next jump solution. Prepare for jump in twenty and acknowledge."

"*Shiny Tin Can acknowledges. I really appreciate traveling with you, you know? Much faster and smoother. How can I persuade you to teach my pilot a few of your tricks?*"

"Ask my skipper, Simon."

The other ships' replies came quick. After two unbelievable seven-sigma jumps in a row, they trusted Yusef's solutions, and there was no reason to waste time in an unnamed pivot system.

He rechecked his own solution anyway, double-checked it, and still found no flaw. "Skipper, we're fine."

"You already announced the next jump, Yusef. Go ahead."

He blushed. Indeed, he should have asked for her permission first.

"Yusef?"

"Yes?"

"I appreciate initiative in my crew. You were ready to accept that responsibility and took it. I'm fine with that. Don't hesitate to ask me whenever you spot something odd, don't trust your own judgment, or just need my reassurance, but as long as you're confident, act. You're a warship pilot now."

Warship pilot. Heck, I hadn't thought of that.

"Crew and guests, prepare for a smooth jump in five."

Harmony beamed at them in bright orange. Yusef only spared it a brief glance before focusing on his routine tasks.

Again, the merchants had arrived in perfect formation. The immediate vicinity showed no obstacles. Harmony One, the planet, ran along its orbit where it should. Everything seemed okay to him.

"Yusef, you have the bridge. Proceed toward Harmony One as scheduled."

"You're leaving?"

"Yes. I'll question our two special guests."

"Oh. Okay."

She left the bridge, and he started checking the readings of their entourage. This frigate's sensors were far more sophisticated than any hauler's.

"*Carthago*, I read a minor jitter in your aft emitters. You might want to check that while we're here."

The merchant confirmed a little while later. "*Thank you — Yusef, right? I'll let my engineer have a look.*"

"You're welcome. I'll announce our arrival now."

He switched. "Harmony port authority. This is Yusef, pilot

of Duchy frigate *Bumblebee* calling. We're escorting a convoy of fifteen haulers from Corfu, two with freight for Harmony. Please acknowledge."

While he waited for their answer, he prepared a solution for an inbound course for their entire convoy, rechecked it, and then sent it out.

"Bumblebee, *this is Harmony port authority. You're highly welcome. We rarely have visitors here. But please explain — we didn't register your reentries. Why?"*

"Harmony, we did a very smooth jump in formation. Your scanners may have missed it."

No merchant objected — they all accepted his proposal. He reconfirmed and set *Bumblebee's* course accordingly.

He began to appreciate the frigate's swiftness. Even if he had to be considerate of the slower haulers, he imagined he could feel the warship's power.

"Bumblebee, *you're not telling me you did a single jump with sixteen merchant ships in formation? Nobody does that."*

Yusef smiled. "We did, Harmony. My skipper believes in precision. You will see."

He watched the merchants assume their positions in a new formation — an idea that had occurred to him before the last jump — and then simultaneously unfold their sails together with *Bumblebee.*

I wouldn't have expected such a bunch of individualists executing my proposal to the letter.

"Nice job, Yusef," Captain Hopper commented. *"Must be quite impressive from outside."*

"We'll know soon enough."

Indeed, the reaction didn't take long.

"Bumblebee, *this is Harmony port authority. Thank you for that outstanding demonstration of precision. Many of us are quite eager now to meet your skipper. Would you please forward some invitations?"*

"Sure."

CHAPTER FORTY-THREE

Syreen would rather not have docked at Harmony Orbital, for three reasons. Firstly, she had no business there, nor had her guests and crew. Secondly, the station and its six docks were in poor condition. Thirdly, she would have saved the harbor fees.

The third argument was vaporized by a generous invitation to dock opposite the old customs and rescue boat.

With her frigate, two docked merchants unloading, two docked ships in need of repairs, and eleven crews having arrived by shuttle, the small orbital station was crowded. The same applied to the harbor master's meeting room. Regularly furnished for up to twelve people, now with hastily added chairs, it hosted fifteen merchant captains, five Harmony officials including the harbor master, and herself—the only woman.

Harmony Orbital was no place for females. On her way from the dock, she'd had plenty of opportunities to notice young women in skimpy frocks doing the work of probably broken cleaning and transport robots while trying to avoid eye contact with males.

I can't save the entire galaxy from such malpractices. I have a mission. They have a mission, too, and they're obviously good at it — this station is in much better shape than Corfu Orbital. Still, it makes me sad to see them suffer. But what can I do?

The locals' emotions were hard to bear, as well. They despised her as a woman in uniform, but couldn't ignore her position as commandant of a warship. Even less could they ignore the guns she carried.

The merchants' respect, or even admiration, was a relief. Not just the two she had saved from the pirates' grip, but all of them were grateful for her escorting skills, and they didn't care at all about her gender.

The harbor master already regretted his invitation, but it couldn't be undone. She was here, in his meeting room, sitting at his table, drinking his forwine.

He tried his best to ignore her by addressing all the other captains, not once talking to her directly. However, her clients did a better job of including her.

"Indeed," Captain Aziz said. "Our readings leave no room for doubt. The shot would have hit. Syreen, how did you manage to dodge it?"

She smiled at Aziz and their host. "I felt something coming and pulled the stick, so that their shot missed. That wasn't the first time—otherwise I wouldn't have been able to collect these." She pointed at the rows of stars on her uniform chest. "Each star stands for a successful kill."

Aziz leaned forward to her. "I count—thirty-seven? All pirates?"

"No. One pirate, twenty-nine stingships, seven larger ships."

Their host clapped his hands. "Sirs, can we talk about business now? What kind of goods have you brought?"

Syreen sensed his embarrassment. A female warship commandant was difficult to ignore, and a successful one . . . before this dissonance of facts and preconceptions could make him do something foolish, she had better fade from his conscious perception, and from those around, too. *Ignore me.*

CHAPTER FORTY-FOUR

Mo watched his skipper eating small bits, chewing them thoroughly, one by one, with no sign of appetite, as though she was performing a disliked chore. They were alone on the bridge, with Yusef and Haiki both asleep in their quarters.

He didn't ask questions. No need to interrupt her, no need to make it harder for her. He just waited until she finished her last bit.

"Worried?" he asked.

"Yes." She shook her head. "I've seen things I should have stopped. Harmony is a bad place. In fact, worse than Corfu."

"Worse? But it looks quite peaceful."

"A graveyard looks quite peaceful, too. Corfu is a rough place, especially for women, but they are open about it. Harmony is a cesspit — and they conceal it well."

"What are you talking about? Abuse? You know, women in space — "

"Are underprivileged or openly exploited, yes. But even ship's cats made their own decision. On Harmony, women are nothing."

"Slaves?"

"Slaves are valuable workers. Sometimes sex workers, but still valuable. On Harmony, nobody asks questions if you mistreat one for nothing."

"What happened?"

"Actually, not much. Initially, they did their best to ignore me, didn't welcome or address me, didn't offer me a chair or

146

a glass of forwine. I can live with that, it only adds to the story. Later, a female servant brought forwine. She wore a cheap frock, was half starved, with bruises and scratches everywhere, didn't dare to look up, and when one of the locals laughed out loud, she flinched and almost spilled the wine — and that in turn triggered a wave of terror in her you could almost hear. No, nothing happened to her, but what I could read in her face plus the malice our hosts radiated says volumes."

"And what are you going to do about it?"

"Now? Nothing. Whatever I could do now would make things worse once we left. Unless I want to castrate and mutilate every single male on Harmony, women's liberation must wait."

"Until . . ."

Finally, she smiled. "Until I return with convincing arguments."

"What kind of arguments?"

"Let's say, a brigade of female marine infantry, armed with cat o' nine tails."

CHAPTER FORTY-FIVE

"Next stop Santana. Fifteen acknowledgments for my solution. We're ready to jump," Yusef said. "You're sure?"

His skipper nodded. "I'm absolutely sure. Sure that your double-seven-sigma solution is perfect. Sure that some pirates in the next pivot system will be terribly disappointed—because we won't even give them time to say hello. Yes, I'm sure we should do it as planned."

"Fine." He switched. "*Bumblebee,* Yusef speaking. Prepare for jump sequence in ten and acknowledge. Crew and guests, prepare for smooth jump in ten."

He focused on his board again. This ship offered so many more options than a hauler—the finest long-range sensors, powerful emitters, classified star catalog entries, and guns—and if he should become its pilot, he would learn how to make best use of them all. So he placed alerts on every escorted merchant's readings, pre-programmed evasion and assault maneuvers, and calculated shooting solutions—which he then safely locked away.

"Check Santana," his skipper said. "Where would you wait for haulers if you wanted to catch one?"

He turned around. "You mean, as a pirate?"

She shrugged and smiled. "Pirate, privateer, corsair, logistics raider, whatever—where'd be your favorite place? Quick—time's running out."

"Oh."

Yusef called up a map of the Santana system, with their

entry point marked, added their best trajectory toward Santana, and computed several interception courses.

Before Syreen could ask the logical next question, he prepared preliminary firing solutions for each of these courses.

That's what I'd expect from my pilot next, if I were skipper. In fact, I should've thought of it before.

There was little time left, but he also programmed several evasion maneuvers—including some counterattack patterns.

"As if you'd done that all your life," Syreen commented.

"Thank you."

There was no time to feel proud. He focused on his readings, as *Bumblebee* jumped, once, twice.

No raiders were waiting for them. Everything else was exactly like on his map—each ship of their convoy where it should be.

"Great job, Yusef," Syreen said. "I'd say you're due for a break."

"Thanks, Skipper. Just let me recheck our inbound course."

"Sure. Just don't let Chiara wait too long."

He sighed inward.

Chiara was a nice girl, too nice for the career she had chosen, pretty, cuddly, skilled, everything a man could ask for in bed, everything a sailor could hope for—but she wasn't like Syreen.

She was and would always be the second choice. It wasn't fair, but she was all he could get, and he'd give her all he could give.

CHAPTER FORTY-SIX

Mo found his captain alone on the bridge. Her gaze seemed to be fixed on some point far outside the ship.

He hesitated to disturb her.

She looked up and smiled. "It's okay. I was listening to Chengdu's song."

"The star?"

"It's lonely. Like them all."

Mo shook his head. "You claimed to hear them before, and I've heard you mention the same to other people, but it still sounds like something imaginary to me."

"I can't make you hear it, so I can't make you believe me."

"Yes—it only bothers me that your claim evades any rational explanation."

"The rational explanation is that I'm a Navigator."

"With capital N, yes. However, until I understand all the implications of that name, it doesn't really strike home."

"Of course. However, until I've come to terms with all the implications myself, and can back them up with some facts, I can't give you a better explanation."

"How can you not know?"

"I never met my parents. I was raised by Fleet. I'm still learning what it means to be a Navigator."

"Oh. I'm sorry to hear that."

"Thank you. It means there's no one I could ask what I am. I have to find out myself. I found out I have a knack with faster-than-light navigation, I can hear the stars sing, and a few other things."

"You're not telling me all."

"No."

"It's okay, you don't have to. Only—if you want to, I'm there."

"I know. I appreciate your loyalty, Mo. At the end of this journey, I'll tell you more."

Mo smiled and cocked his head. "You know, I'm curious. I want to know the whole story. And I'm not the only one. You've noticed no merchant left us at Zamora—no one to take the return route to Corfu, despite that smooth seven-sigma four-jump sequence Yusef offered."

"Yes—I already wondered why."

"Hah—if they've learned one thing by now, it's that they're part of something special. No, something unique. Eight systems, seventeen seven-sigma jumps, ten of which came in pairs, one as a triple—their emitters should be smoking from the strain, but instead are as fresh as new ones. You dodge pulse shots, keep them safe, and make them earn more money they could have planned for. Meanwhile, they all carry goods for the next stops, and they can expect a warm welcome on planets long neglected. Harbor masters are asking questions—*who's that woman registered as star angel for the third time now? Who's that woman protecting you? Who's that woman letting you make jumps we can't detect? Who's that woman acting like she owns the whole galaxy?* No, it's no longer just about the money, it's about being part of something way greater. They only can't see the whole picture yet." He shrugged. "Nor can I."

"Somehow I missed that third registration."

"Captain Palmer recorded it at Harmony. Guess why."

"I can imagine." She added a weak smile. "That wasn't what you came for."

"No. We'll soon be ready to travel. Are you still considering a detour to Second Stop?"

"Yes and no. The next leg will be the most difficult, not as smooth as the ones before. To reach Nizwa, we must do a few low-quality jumps."

"How low?"

"Five-sigma, at least twice."

"Oh, and I thought it'd be bad. Five-sigma is nothing."

"Yes — but that's the route through Second Stop. The other solutions are worse."

"Really?"

"Yes. That's what the songs tell me — the spacetime continuum is damaged between Chengdu and Nizwa, like a rift in space. There is no reasonable detour."

Mo nodded. "I've heard of such rifts. Merchants try to avoid them."

"The explorers did a good job charting this area, so you can navigate around the worst ruptures, and the safest passage is the one through Second Stop. No surprise — the other two pivot systems are called First Stop and Third Stop, and we're doing them in reverse order."

"So we can't avoid going there?"

"I had hoped to find a different route once we were closer, but no. We could return to Corfu and forget about the other side, but I won't do that. For one, my final destination is behind the rift. For two, our merchants carry goods for Nizwa and beyond. I promised I'd get them there, and I'll keep my promise."

"By taking them to a pirate's nest."

"No. There will be no pirate's nest anymore."

CHAPTER FORTY-SEVEN

Syreen closed her eyes, took a deep breath and held it. With her fingers wrapped around the flight stick, she missed the strength of another firm stick inside her, she missed the tight fit of a skirmisher seat or *Assiduous'* comforting hug.

No psyjuice this time, no deep integration. Her skills, and a little help from her beast, would have to make the difference.

Bumblebee was going into battle. In her announcement, she hadn't left room for any doubt about it. The fifteen haulers had to stay behind, and her girls had to stay behind, too.

At this point of their journey, her request hadn't met resistance. The merchant captains had offered her girls hospitality — as guests, not as ship's cats — until they rejoined. Neither had they asked for compensation, nor had any of them voiced reservations regarding their safety.

"Jump in two," Yusef announced. "You have the ship."

"I have the ship."

She opened her senses. Third Stop's song faded into the background. *Bumblebee's* emitters began to weave their jump field around the ship.

The frigate penetrated the hyperplane, dashed forward through the torn and stirred continuum, and reentered spacetime in a blink.

Short-range sensors picked up gravitational and electromagnetic emissions, recognized the patterns of charged guns, and triggered alarm.

Yes, seen that, on it.

153

Syreen aimed and released one of her guns, only then pulling her stick to one side.

A hostile shot missed.

She switched her attention to the long-range sensors, prioritized two more targets, and fired again. This time, the packets of coherent high-energy photons had to travel farther.

Two more symbols turned purple.

"Yes!" Yusef yelled.

Syreen focused on a new threat that *Bumblebee* was just about to spot—two emitter-driven missiles.

Nasty little beasts.

"Incoming missiles!" Yusef hurried to provide her with evasion options.

She fired instead. One shot hit home, the other missed its target when the missile danced its own evasion pattern.

Her follow-up blasted it away, and *Bumblebee's* next salvo vaporized the pirate hauler those missiles had come from.

The frigate flipped around. Now she could bring her pair of cold rear guns to bear.

One pirate had cut his reactor and was opening his sails as a sign of surrender. The other remained a legitimate target.

Syreen couldn't know whether either of them carried missiles, too. Launching missiles didn't require a hot reactor, so both of her targets were potential threats.

The second still hadn't offered visible signs of surrender.

Your bad.

A double shot eliminated that risk. Next, she flipped ship again and gave her stick a nudge. *Bumblebee* gracefully swayed away from a powerful laser beam.

Capacitor driven? So much for your surrender.

Without remorse, she triggered two of her forward guns again, and destroyed the last enemy ship.

Six kills. I won't waste a tear on this scum.

Neither short-range sensors nor long-range sensors, not even her own senses, unveiled more current threats. She allowed herself to relax, stretch her tensed muscles, and take another deep breath.

Yusef kept his focus on the board, but issued a *Phew*.

Only now could she check for incoming calls. *Bumblebee* had recorded a few older ones, asking for her surrender, and one current emergency call.

"Shoot again?" Yusef asked.

"Of course not. If there are survivors, they'll face a court-martial. After that, I'll gladly execute each of them." She smiled. "Thank you, Yusef. Your preparations were spot-on. The first two pirates had picked the same positions you expected—only they weren't as precise as expected."

"Thank you."

"And we both wouldn't have thought there'd be so many of them, eh, Yusef?"

"No—and I wouldn't have thought you could shoot two short-range missiles before they hit us."

This time, he glanced over his shoulder, and she gave him a mischievous smile. "The closer they come, the easier they are to hit."

"Do you get stars for those birds, too?"

"No. Only for the ships."

CHAPTER FORTY-EIGHT

When the call came, Syreen was ready. She nodded at Mo, who had taken Yusef's place on the bridge, and leaned back.

"Unknown warship for Second Stop harbor master, please explain your destination and intentions."

She shook her head. Were they unable to read transponder codes?

"Second Stop, this is Duchy frigate *Bumblebee,* Fleet Commander Syreen speaking. We're clearing the way as escort for a merchant convoy bound for Woo. Please explain the presence of six illegally armed haulers in your system."

She cut the line and answered Mo's grin in kind.

"How creative will they be?" he asked.

"Hopefully very creative," she replied. "I wouldn't like the other option."

"Which would be?"

"Trying to shoot us with long-range missiles to keep us at a distance."

"Oh—that's a scary idea."

"Indeed. Shooting their orbital station's missile bay across several light minutes should put some fear into their hearts."

Mo raised his eyebrows. "Even warship guns can't be effective across that distance."

"That's what the Books say. I don't play by the Books."

"No, and the laws of physics can't stop you, either."

"In this case, it's all about precision. If I can make our four forward guns hit in the same place, there will be a notable

156

effect. If I flip the ship around and add two more hits from the aft guns right after, there will be a significant effect. However, that'll mean extra work for Haiki."

The merchant captain nodded. "I understand. Such high-energy shots would overheat the guns and disarm us."

"No. Only an unlikely follow-up shot without prior maintenance would disarm us, otherwise I couldn't risk such a gamble in a pirate hub." She pointed at her board. "We'll know soon—if they really want to fight, they must start before we're too close."

"In their place, I'd carefully check the readings from our battle before engaging us. The way you handled those bogeys and their missiles was very instructive."

"Yes. The alternative would have been our very instructive end. I had to be quick."

"They were well prepared, with their missiles and all—they must have expected to win."

"An ambush with six gunships against a single escort ship like ours is a safe bet. You'd need at least a cruiser to take a beating and get away."

"But you refused to take the beating. They couldn't know we have a Navigator—or what that means."

"But they knew we were coming."

"Yes." Mo shook his head. "Things are changing for the worse. Back when I was an apprentice pilot, routes were safe, and pirates were just old lore."

"That's what my instructors told me—however, the Duchy had a strict zero-tolerance policy regarding pirates. That's what they told me, too. Why do you have to teach zero tolerance for old lore to young recruits? That doesn't add up."

"Indeed." The old merchant captain scratched his chin. "Well—in the old days, we traveled everywhere, the AP, the old colonies, the outer rim, the lost and found worlds, and never met pirates. I felt safe. Pirates were history, nothing more. But by and by, that changed. We heard of an encounter on a less-frequented route, of another in a remote area, a wild story from the rim . . . and one day, the guild published new recommendations for safe travel. Suddenly it was official — pirates exist. From there, things went down the drain." He sighed. "Recently, the descent's speeding up. Pirates operating at fleet strength — what's next?"

Syreen made a grim face. "Pirates operating warships are the logical next step. It won't be this one, though."

She checked her panel. "Almost time for their next call."

They had to wait for another centicycle until the panel signaled another incoming transmission.

"Almost in time," Syreen commented and grinned at Mo before she pulled it up.

"*Duchy frigate* Bumblebee, *this is Second Stop harbor master. You're not escorting anyone. Instead, you shot six civil ships immediately upon arrival in our system. Be instructed that our long-range defense is already locked on your ship. Turn away and leave, or face the consequences.*"

Mo shook his head. "They didn't check their readings."

"Not really." Syreen focused on her panel.

"Second Stop, this is *Bumblebee* again. You failed to explain the presence of six illegally armed, repeat, armed haulers. Your readings could have told you they were shooting this frigate immediately upon arrival. They shot first, without issuing a warning. The Duchy has a strict no-tolerance policy on piracy, so I eliminated this threat. I strongly advise you to consider your next actions and check what I did with the short-range missiles launched at me. I will treat any assault without prior declaration of war as piracy and eliminate the originator. You're receiving my reply on a tight beam — be assured I can aim my guns as precisely as my radio. And, on the topic of escorting, check your readings again — now."

She had her timing right. With her last words, the first

merchants dropped out of hyperspace, and the last only a blink after she had finished.

"That should give them something to think about," Mo said.

"If they have the tools to think," she answered. "Now, would you please welcome our herd and advise them of the situation? Unless they need urgent maintenance, I'd like to leave as soon as possible."

"I'm sure they're not eager to stay here. I'll talk with them."

Syreen watched Mo retrieving fresh readings of the haulers' emitters. He'd check for any glitches they might have missed. She directed her attention to her own board, locked a few alarms on the planet and its orbital station, and turned her chair to the wall. Whatever the local authorities intended to do, they would need time.

Meanwhile, she focused on Second Stop's song. As all the stars before, it sang of loneliness, of the slow passing of time, of resource consumption and the inevitable decline, but also of the joy of burning and shining.

By and by she tuned in to it, resonated and answered its song. The deeper she went, the more harmonics she recognized. The star told her how it felt to be trapped in this rift, surrounded by ripped space. It harbored and shared a vast amount of detail about the structure of space and hyperspace, about the structure of the rift and its rips and tides, and in the deeper harmonies, she even found hints of how the damage had developed over the last gigacycles.

One day, I'll have a deeper look into that. Who knows, perhaps we can do something about it?

159

CHAPTER FORTY-NINE

Mo cut the line and turned around. "Fifteen acknowledgments. We're ready to go."

Syreen nodded. "Okay." She switched to the intercom. "Prepare for jump in ten. Crew and guests, prepare for jump in ten."

Mo waved outward. "They've sent their thanks—the last jump was a five-plus, wasn't it? Smoother than expected."

"Yes. I think I learned something about the rift. The better you understand it, the better your solution can be."

He grinned. "And next time, you do seven-sigma around here?"

He thought he was teasing her, but she replied, "Certainly. However, it won't work for a convoy. I could only do it for my own ship."

"Because you'd be flying with your ass?"

"Close, Mo. Very close."

What was she hiding behind that smile? More secrets?

One day she'll tell me.

"Prepare for trouble ahead," she said. "We're not done yet."

"What do you expect?"

"Anything. You know, the two pirate crews of *Veronica's Smile* and *Athabasca* couldn't have expected to get all the other thirteen ships under control."

"So there are more to come."

"Yes and no. Those could be behind us. With our double-jump sequences we might have outrun them, or they might

160

have passed us while our haulers were transshipping. No — either they're behind us, on the other side of the rift, or they were part of that six-ship pack at Second Stop."

"Yes. I wonder what it is about that system anyway."

"Oh, that's easy to figure out. It's a relatively safe place in the rift, and it must have been quite frequented in the past. Ships traveling from Zamora or Chengdu to Nizwa or back have to pass there. You've noticed their orbital station?"

"I only had a brief look at the readings."

"It's larger than you'd expect in such a remote place. The reason are its docks and maintenance facilities — perfectly suited for fixing damages caused by traveling the rift. In the past, they must have been busy — plus, they're well equipped to defend themselves with their long-range missiles. With the increase of pirate activities, they're out of business, though — because this route is the perfect place for ambushes. Everyone must pass through First, Second and Third Stop. So, when no more merchants came, they became the ideal place for pirates to dock and repair. I don't know how the pirates took over, but — well, all their gun-and-missile armament isn't worth a credit once a ship has docked. So now they are that pirate hub no one goes to. But there's still travel on both sides of the rift, and occasionally even across — I wonder why some of our skippers accepted freight for the other side. Weren't they aware of the rift?"

"From what they said, they were trying a new route. Some-one proposed good business to them."

"Indeed. Good business — by luring them on a pirate route."

"They figured out something like that when they arrived at Corfu. That's why they didn't dare to travel on. Until you came along."

"Until we came along, yes. In any case, I expect as many pirates lying in wait on the other side of the rim as where we came from. Perhaps even in the Nizwa system. Which we will find out right after this jump."

"Oh. So we better get ready."

"Yes. However, we have an advantage—they won't notice our seven-sigma jump shock until it's too late."

"Any pirates will be in for an even bigger surprise." Mo grinned as he imagined it. Only for a moment, then he focused on his board. Should there be any danger, Syreen would handle the immediate situation, and he'd make sure there'd be no nasty surprises later.

CHAPTER FIFTY

The small customs boat watching the primary riftside arrival point suddenly faced a frigate with hot guns and active target acquisition sensors.

Its skipper decided not to shoot first.

Syreen sighed with relief. *Good. I wouldn't be eager shooting people only doing their duty, even in self-defense.*

She activated her radio. "Nizwa authorities, this is Duchy frigate *Bumblebee,* Fleet Commander Syreen speaking. I'm escorting a convoy of fifteen haulers across the rift. My protégées will arrive with short delay and in tight formation. Due to recent pirate activity, I'm advancing to clear the situation. Some of our haulers carry goods for Nizwa."

The reply came quick. "Bumblebee, *this is Nizwa customs gunboat* Tall Guard. *I'm First Lieutenant Majowsky. We're glad to welcome a friendly escort to Nizwa, and we're grateful for any information on recent pirate activity. Can you give us a brief initial summary, while we assume you'll accompany your convoy to Nizwa?"*

"Sure, First Lieutenant Majowsky. We eliminated two pirates after leaving Corfu and six pirate vessels armed with guns and short-range missiles at Second Stop. For the moment, the path through the rift might be clear."

"Your frigate seems undamaged. Or do you need any assistance?"

I'd tell you right away if I did, sure. Syreen smiled. "We might consider picking up provisions if you have any local produce to spare. Otherwise, we're fine, thank you."

163

"Glad to hear that. You mentioned you're fleet commander. What rank exactly is that within the Duchy?"

"It's superior to admiral—it means I'm supreme commander of the entire Duchy Navy. However, I had to give up my flagship for a secret mission. That's why I acquired this frigate."

"Oh, yes, according to our records, it's an AP warship."

"It was. I captured it. The Duchy is at war with the AP."

"You dared to attack the AP?"

"No. The AP dared to attack us, without prior declaration of war. Thousands of civilians died in the initial wave."

"You're fighting back with a single frigate."

"Not exactly. Before, I only had a corvette, but so far, I've eliminated thirty-six AP ships, including six tanks and one dreadnaught."

"A corvette? I think we heard stories about a corvette recently."

"Maybe you heard about the *Light of Mandalay*."

"We did. There, a corvette was involved."

"It was my corvette."

There was a brief pause. *"You're the star angel, then. I'm honored to meet you."*

"You're welcome to meet me in person, any time."

"Oh, I'm not due for relief yet. I have to keep my station. But thank you for the offer. Another time, perhaps. I'd say you're always welcome at Nizwa."

CHAPTER FIFTY-ONE

Syreen gave her staff captain an encouraging smile. "Relax, Mo. Try to enjoy the invitation. You're not going to a funeral."

He shrugged and tried a smile himself. "I know. I guess the events at Second Stop are still haunting me. Or starting to haunt me, now that I feel the relief of having arrived in a safer place."

"If it helps, I'm the one who should worry."

"You? Why?"

"By now, the story about our encounter between Corfu and Harmony should be going around, so the AP knows where their lost frigate is. Of our merchants, I can't tell who told what to whom, but our scheduled route might have been leaked. By doing our double-seven jumps, we might stay ahead of pursuers, but each transshipping eats away at our head start. And the AP may well decide to send a battle group to each of the systems we yet have to visit. Should they find us, things will get nasty."

"You could still surrender."

"No, I couldn't, for reasons I can't explain yet. But I *can* deal with an AP battle group." She pointed at the hatch, now signaling breathable air on its other side. "And I can deal with a dinner invitation. Let's go."

Five people were waiting for them once they entered the dock. Syreen sensed only friendliness and walked up to them, unsure who to address first.

165

"Fleet Commander Syreen, welcome to Nizwa Orbital," the pretty young woman in the fashionable red jumpsuit with its daringly deep cleavage said and reached out a hand. "I'm Juanita, Nizwa harbor master."

She had a firm grip. Syreen wasn't used to handshakes, but Juanita's felt comfortable. "My staff captain Mo."

Mo and Juanita shook hands, too.

Their host gestured to an older man in a gray suit, a pad tucked under his arm. "Orville, secretary of the merchant guild."

Orville shook Syreen's hand first. "I'm honored to meet the first-ever double star angel in person. We're grateful for your efforts for free and safe trade all around space."

A nudge by Juanita stopped him.

He nodded and turned to Mo.

Juanita waved three people in uniforms forward. With their white trousers, red jackets, white caps, and lots of ornaments, they didn't look like soldiers to Syreen, but she sensed their professional attitude. Their salute was flawless, as was her reply.

Perhaps their shiny style is meant to distract?

"Lieutenant Matthew, Private Hannah, Private Peter, your personal assistants during your stay. Whatever you need, they'll take care of it."

Whatever we need? Well, they sure look tasty.

"I'm sure you've already taken care of anything we might need," she said.

Juanita smiled. "Of course. May I ask you to follow me?"

"Sure."

While she followed their host, Syreen contemplated the striking differences between the last destinations. After Corfu and Harmony, she had expected things to take a turn for the worse. However, Santana had simply been poor yet tidy. Backwater hadn't lived up to its name, with its sophisticated cultural performances. Kumasi had been strict and spartan, but tidy and clean as well. Quito and Pompeii had been much like Corfu, Zamora even worse, and Chengdu a mix between Harmony and Kumasi—strict and no place for women. Nizwa was a positive surprise, and it reminded her of Kyris or her home, despite its remote location.

"Are you okay?" Juanita asked.

Syreen found genuine worry in her face.

"Old memories," she explained. "It's been a while since I've felt so welcome anywhere. It reminds me of home."

"Oh—thank you."

Obviously, business talk was generally frowned upon at the dinner table. Whenever one of the skippers insinuated anything toward serious topics, or even openly tried to touch on it, one of their hosts would interrupt him.

To spare them any further embarrassment, Syreen gave those too enthusiastic a gentle mental nudge. Didn't they notice that by listening to small talk about their meal, about local culture and entertainment, about their hosts' garments and accessories, they could learn a lot about local goods and needs?

From their chat she concluded Nizwa had a solid agricultural as well as industrial base, way above the minimum standard for self-sufficient operation that had been compulsory for any long-term colonization. They could afford state-of-the-art engineering and electronics, cheap commuting including surface-to-orbit travel, basic social security for the entire populace.

"We're wealthy enough that we don't have to treat anyone as underprivileged," Orville explained. "Of course, people must contribute to get anything but their basic needs covered—whether they run errands for those who can't, perform arts for the public, or produce goods. Everything anyone considers useful counts."

Juanita winked at him.

"What kind of entertainment do you like most, Fleet Commander Syreen?" Orville quickly changed the subject.

"Oh, please call me Syreen. Entertainment—uh, sure, I, well, I like sharing passion."

"I don't understand?"

"Making love."

Orville blushed, but only slightly, then he joined in with the laughter all around.

The lounge seemed to be the place for business. They had only just moved there from dinner, and had provided Syreen with another forwine, when Orville approached her, a few other men with gray temples in his wake.

"Syreen, may I ask you about your plans for the future?"

He must have instantly sensed her disinclination to unveil her plans, or he had recognized his own bad phrasing, because in either case, he continued, "What kind of good news may we expect from our star angel in the near future?"

Again, there was a lot she didn't want to tell them, but when she was asked this way, she could answer in more general terms. Her final goal was no secret, after all.

"You may have heard, or more likely haven't, how my mission began—with an unprecedented atrocity, with a massacre to the thousands of civil staff and visitors aboard the Duchy's orbital station when it was destroyed without prior warning. There was no advance declaration of war before the AP fleet led by Vice Admiral Cornelius Ravenport aboard the dreadnaught *APS Illustrious* murdered them all."

Shock and disbelief showed in their faces. Conversations around her froze, and all attention turned toward her. Her *personal assistants* moved closer with curious faces, too.

"I have sufficient telemetry data to prove my charge of piracy. In the following course of events, as the most senior survivor of Duchy Fleet, I became Fleet Commander in Charge, and as such I am entitled to follow up on this crime according to universal laws and standing Duchy regulations against piracy. I am entitled to declare and conduct war against the Associated Planets, and I will teach them a lesson."

Juanita was the first to point out the obvious. "With a single frigate?"

Syreen showed her a smile that made the harbor master step back. "I've already taken out one of their dreadnaughts, one battle cruiser, and a destroyer with my bare hands. I assure you, this war will not be won by quantities."

"I'm suddenly very curious how you acquired your current ship. You know it once was registered as an AP frigate?"

"I'm aware of that. I decided to change its ownership. It was basically a question of walking in and throwing the original crew out."

"On your own. Sounds hard to believe."

Captain Palmer moved forward. "As hard to believe as her walking into my ship and praising away the pirates who had held us hostage. From what I've seen so far, I'm inclined to believe anything she says and ask myself what else she held back."

Juanita nodded and focused on her. "Seems you've done a good job for these guys. Merchants usually don't volunteer any praise that could cause a raise, or what was that proverb?"

Palmer smiled. "Almost right. However, merchants usually don't travel with an escort commander who dares to jump right into a trap and comes out without as much as a scratch. I've watched her recordings—they were already waiting for us at Second Stop."

"I heard you eliminated six pirates at Second Stop. I assumed they were spread across the system," Juanita said.

Palmer shook his head. "Nay—they were assembled around the arrival point from Third Stop. They obviously knew we were coming eventually, and when our frigate came out of the jump, they fired."

"Poor shooters, then."

"From the data I've seen, the shot came right on target from closest distance—only she dodged it. Like she did before."

Palmer nodded at her.

Orville frowned. "That could almost sound like it was staged—sorry, no offense meant."

"You're right," Syreen said. "It could almost sound staged—if it were possible to stage coming out of a jump and dodging the first shot within millicycles—after shooting the originator—without prior syncing. It was no easy feat anyway. Moreover I doubt any pirate would volunteer for such a suicide mission."

"Any other explanation would be even more unlikely. No one can dodge a short-range gun shot. After all, those travel at light speed. You can't see and react." Orville shook his head. "What happened there? A little exaggeration perhaps, out of excitement?"

"You may check the recordings," Syreen said. "Everything he says is true."

Orville spread his arms. "From everything I know, it can't be."

"You don't know all. I could sense the shot when it was fired—at the very same moment, not limited by light speed."

"Impossible."

"For ordinary humans, yes. I'm a Navigator." *As if that would explain anything for them.*

The guild secretary only stared at her. She could sense the uproar in his mind. *What does he know?*

After two deep breaths, he had regained his composure and bowed. "We are blessed."

"What does that mean?" Juanita asked.

"That she's telling the truth. She *can* do what she claims."

Juanita turned to Mo. "What does that mean?"

"She's a Navigator. She does the smoothest jumps, she dodges shots fast as light, and she can hear the stars sing. She can bring a frigate dirtside and back into space. She never misses her target. Those are the major points, I think."

Their host rolled her eyes. "Men!"

For a moment, Syreen thought she felt the attention turning away from her. The merchant skippers were discussing the marketability of local products.

However, Juanita quickly grabbed the opportunity to talk with her alone. "I figure your next stop is Puerto La Cruz."

"Yes, that's correct."

"I guess that's a significant choice — they're always in need of everything. Not because they're poor, but they're messy and never get things done. However, those things they *do* get done are sought after on many worlds, as far as I've heard. Will you eventually return here?"

The sudden change of topic couldn't surprise Syreen. "Probably. I've learned the stars around the rift are kind of pirate infested. Those provide a splendid opportunity for shooting practice — plenty of reasons to return." She grinned. "On the other hand, should my intention become known to a wider public, pirates might choose to keep a rather low profile or entirely avoid the area."

The harbor master raised her eyebrows. "Some people might be interested in spreading such news. People like merchants or harbor masters. Scaring pirates away would be a good thing for them — and their purses."

"You might happen to know such people? I should be careful who I talk to lest my secret plans become unveiled." *While I'd very much appreciate the AP searching for me in all the wrong places.* She shrugged and grinned. "On the other hand, knowing my friends were safe would put my mind at ease — while

I'm chasing and shooting pirates elsewhere."

Not to mention the fact that a massed AP presence hereabouts won't be good for pirate business either.

"It would, however, reduce the likelihood of your return."

"For a while, yes, but if I don't follow up on my announcement, they might return faster than we'd all like, and in strength. I couldn't let that happen. So, in general, I do indeed plan my return—whether to Nizwa or to Harmony is a different question."

Juanita made a face. "Harmony? Bad place, why would you want to return there, of all possible destinations?"

"To make a change for the better, for the women there."

Syreen began to report her observations. Although she refrained from adding her conclusions, Juanita paled—at first, then Syreen felt the anger rise in the harbor master, and it felt much like her own beast. For all she could tell however, Juanita was an ordinary human.

Perhaps my beast is just that—unvented anger. Add my canines and a natural demand for highly nutritive human blood, and the label sticks.

When she finished her report, Juanita had calmed down again.

The harbor master gazed past her. "It is so . . . unusual to meet someone who cares so much beyond her obligations and personal acquaintances. Why do you burden yourself with such issues?"

Syreen shrugged. "Because I can? I guess it's because I don't want to live in an environment that doesn't care."

Juanita pursed her lips. "Well."

She balanced on her toes for a moment. "Well."

The harbor master looked around, then focused on Syreen again. "Well. I will talk with some people and send a few messages. I don't have many friends on other worlds, but . . . let's see what I can do. I will gather supporters for you, and if . . . when you return to Nizwa, I will accompany you to

Harmony, together with anyone who's ready to help, too. Whatever needs to be done, we'll do it. Including the worrisome part of justifying our intervention—no doubt, such treatment of females is against established interstellar conventions, at least as long as a world isn't interdicted, which they aren't—but you can't simply go there and mess with an independent world."

"Thank you. I appreciate your offer, and I also appreciate your legal concern. However, I assure you, I *can* simply go there and mess with their bloody independent world. I'll explain that once I return, and you've now given me a very good reason to return. May the stars always sing happy songs for you."

"Huh?"

CHAPTER FIFTY-TWO

"Prepare for double-jump sequence in ten," Yusef announced.

Fingers running across his board, he double-checked his convoy solution once again. Of course, he found no flaw.

Unless their emitters — or those of their merchant flotilla — developed a sudden unexpected and totally unforeseeable flaw, these jumps would be as unspectacular and hardly noticeable as the previous ones, those three from Nizwa to Puerto La Cruz and the double on to Le Mans.

As unspectacular as Le Mans itself. If anything at all, they've invented boredom. I wouldn't mind if I never returned here.

His skipper took a deep breath. He turned around.

"Worried?"

She nodded. "Somewhat. I've expected more pirates to show up at some point. With each jump, I'm prepared for another battle, and then — again, nothing."

"Better to be prepared and disappointed than to be caught with your pants down." The words were out before he realized what he'd said. "Uh — sorry, I mean . . ."

"You're welcome. I've been skirmisher pilot, Yusef. Essentially, I went into battle with my pants down. Being fully dressed in combat is the unfamiliar part of it."

"With your pants down?"

"Figuratively — literally, you fly nude."

"Why?"

"First, there's the psyjuice shot. That's a drug enhancing your reflexes — and it makes you horny. Second, you fly with

174

a stimulator, that way you're rewarded for successful kills. There's no greater incentive than a psyjuice-enhanced orgasm, and that's what makes skirmisher pilots so successful."

Yusef tried hard to resist the imagery.

She smiled. "Yes, even the idea of it is arousing, isn't it? It was fun—as long as it remained a training exercise. It was no longer fun when all my wing mates were shot dead and that enemy cruiser launched its missiles at me. In any case—I have no issues with nudity or talking about it."

Yusef felt relief, and nodded. For the upcoming jump, she'd need a pilot focused on his job, though. So he checked the prepared options on his board.

"Jump in one," Yusef said.

Bumblebee jumped once—all green—and a second time. Again, all indicators remained green. Without strain on their emitters, there was no reason for failures.

Passive scans started automatically.

Syreen sensed a hot prickle and pulled her stick hard. The frigate dashed forward and to the side, and several indicators turned yellow.

Two forward guns fired, the ship shook, turned, and shot again. Red lights flashed on their dashboards. Klaxons wailed, while a bell announced the radar signals of homing missiles. Her board showed two more targets behind them.

With another pull at her stick, she made *Bumblebee* roll and yaw out of the path of another shot. Her own guns shot three missiles and grazed a fourth.

The bell silenced.

The four forward guns fired together, *Bumblebee* flipped, and the rear guns finished off their next target.

The frigate flipped and shot one gun again.

"I don't read any more targets," Yusef said.

"Neither do I," she agreed. "Damage report."

"We have a minor hull breach in section Charlie Four. Haiki is on his way."

Charlie Four — close to the frigate's center, below the center deck. Batteries or spare parts? "Any casualties?"

"No reports yet."

"Keep me posted. Check for navigation hazards, please."

Only now did she find time to examine the plot in detail. Their raiders had been close—too close for her taste.

Four ships had attacked her, a pair of large haulers and two small ones of patrol boat size. With her initial volley she had killed the first patrol boat and damaged one hauler. The quadruple shot had eliminated the second hauler—the missile launcher—and her aft guns had taken the second patrol boat out. The last single shot had finished the damaged hauler off.

"This is new," she mused aloud. "They'd brought two armed patrol boats to this pivot system. Count in the missiles, and they must have had access to military equipment. Plus, their haulers' bridge and reactor sections were reinforced, strong enough to resist our guns."

She spoke up. "Yusef, we'll have to stay in this system for a while. Prepare a safe path for our convoy, staying clear of the debris, and unfold our collectors. Once Haiki is done with the hole, he should look after our guns. I fear I've abused them."

"Better abused than dead," Yusef said. "These four were tough."

"Yes—and thank you for the quick target prioritization. That helped a lot."

Her pilot smiled. "I'm glad I could assist."

"No, really—that was excellent."

CHAPTER FIFTY-THREE

Syreen approached Captain Palmer, one glass of bubbly for-wine in each hand. She had to wiggle her way through the party guests—her female passengers were happily chatting and drinking with the male merchant crews, and the few occasionally disappearing couples didn't improve the situation much in the crowded mess. Kathmandu finally offered the opportunity to celebrate, as she had promised the ladies.

Palmer smiled at her and took the offered glass. "Congratulations! Once again, you've led a brilliant fight. A bit tight this time, wasn't it?"

"Indeed. Without a safe secondary entry point, they could pick the best position. I won't choose such a pivot system again. Makes me too predictable."

"The outcome was predictable, too. I still have no clue how you do it."

"I can't explain it. I know I can dodge those shots, but I don't know how."

"That must be worrisome."

"No." She shook her head. "No, there are too many other subjects I have to worry about. The AP, for example."

"I've heard Mo mention something like that."

"It's a five-jump route to Woo, and Woo is a fairly safe place. I will leave you at the last pivot system and not do the jump to Woo myself. You should be okay—and I won't charge for Woo."

Palmer smiled. "You'd deserve the fee anyway, or a lot more after what you did for us. This time, you even suffered

177

minor damage, right? You could've demanded compensation for that."

"I hadn't expected damage, and your fees cover my docking fees, that's all I need." *As long as this ship reaches its destination in one piece, I'm fine. After that . . . well.*

"You have to pay your crew and feed your guests, too."

"Oh, that's covered, too."

"You shouldn't tell me. Weakens your position."

They smiled at each other knowingly.

"My negotiation skills leave room for improvement."

"Sometimes. I won't complain about your negotiation skills toward pirates, though. I'm grateful, and I owe you. Personally, I mean."

"As long as it doesn't interfere with your business, you mean?" She winked. "Okay, perhaps I may ask you a favor, then."

"Of course."

"Even if Kathmandu seems to have no nasty surprises in for us, I don't want to leave my bridge unguarded, especially my long-range sensors. But I'd like my crew—my entire crew—to join the party for a little ceremony."

The captain raised his eyebrows. "You'd trust your bridge to me?"

"I know I can depend on you. My life in your hands."

He straightened and saluted. "At your service, Ma'am, immediately. I'm honored, I won't disappoint you—and this minor service won't pay my debt."

Syreen returned the salute. *Good man.* She watched him push through the crowd.

Syreen found Haiki tightly wrapped in Gwen's arms, both slowly working their way toward the hallway. By nudging a few others out of her way, either mentally or physically, she managed to intercept them in time.

Haiki made a disappointed face. He obviously had other

things on his mind than a chitchat with his skipper.

"Sorry, Haiki. I've asked Palmer to relieve Yusef on the bridge. Once he's here, I want to make an announcement, and I want to make sure my crew won't miss it. There's still plenty of party time after."

"Oh, okay." He glanced at Gwen.

"Make sure his glass isn't empty," Syreen said to her. "I'll go and find Mo."

"I've seen Jona and him close to the bar," Gwen whispered.

"Thank you." Syreen nodded.

With more nudges and pushes, she approached the bar and soon spotted her staff captain.

"You didn't come to tell me you've got an urgent job for me?" he asked doubtfully.

"In fact, I do." She grinned. "I need an improvised stage — just a table or so, wide enough for four people, in a centicycle or three."

Mo glanced at Jona. "Oh, that's manageable. Karim, would you lend us a hand?"

Carthago's skipper grinned. "Sure, Mo. What for?"

Mo explained the task, and together with Jona, they quickly cleared a small area and brought out one of the tables they had previously stowed away to make room for the party.

They were just finished when Yusef appeared. "You need me, skipper?"

"Yes. Grab a glass and wait for your cue."

"Uh-hum."

From her elevated position on the improvised stage, Syreen could see almost all of her protégées' curious faces — obviously the word had spread around. She didn't have to ask for silence.

"Thank you, folks," she began. "I want to thank you all for the advance trust you gave an unknown frigate captain from a less than well-known star system. Many of you reassured me this investment paid back well, and I don't want to reiterate all the events leading to this assessment. However, I want to point out the last incident—that short battle with two heavily armed and armored haulers and two patrol boats, the closest any pirate so far has come to commanding a warship. The times are changing, and not for the better, it seems. I'm doing what little I can to turn this trend around, and I take any help I can get, volunteered or not. The way I found my current crew was more like the latter—they lost their ship because of my actions, and I offered them new jobs, if only temporary. I've invested my trust in them, in their loyalty, and in their skills, and my investment paid back well, too. Whether it's the way my staff captain deals with an anarchic bunch of pretty passengers, or the fixes my engineer applies with a snap of his fingers, or the jump solutions my pilot provides to all of you, they're demonstrating an extraordinary performance way above their duties, way above what I could reasonably have expected. This is true dedication, and as such must be honored."

She nodded at Mo. "Mo, please come forward, come up here."

Syreen waited until he had climbed the table.

"Ladies and gentlemen. As Duchy Fleet Commander in Charge, it is my duty and pleasure to announce—in recognition of his extraordinary performance, especially in coordinating passenger safety during the most recent battle, with a hull breach in a potentially critical section of this ship, I herewith award you, Mo, the Duchy's Bronze Star for your gallantry."

She pulled the thumb-sized award from her pocket and attached it to Mo's uniform chest under the audience's frenetic applause.

Mo seemed to fight for words. "Gallantry—a medal? Me?"

She patted his back. "Be proud. You earned it."

When his well-deserved applause faded, she nodded at her engineer. "Haiki, please come forward."

Haiki shook his head. He seemed to be too nervous to move so the timid Gwen had to give him a push.

"Yes, Haiki, come up."

She made him stand between Mo and her.

"Ladies and gentlemen. As Duchy Fleet Commander in Charge, it is my duty and pleasure to announce — in recognition of his extraordinary performance, especially in applying an emergency repair to a hull breach, in a vented section of the ship, during an ongoing battle, I herewith award you, Haiki, the Duchy's Silver Star for your gallantry."

As Mo before, she could sense how Haiki fought with his own disbelief. But when she applied the award to his uniform chest, she could watch a change inside him. He straightened not only physically, but also mentally, accepted his own pride, and then radiated it.

Gwen's "Yeees!" drowned out even the roaring applause. Next, she jumped up onto the table and kissed Haiki.

Syreen nodded at Yusef. *Yes, you too.*

Although he didn't need the cue, she said, "Yusef, come forward."

Chiara wasn't far away when he climbed the stage. *Good. He'll need her soon.*

"Ladies and gentlemen. As Duchy Fleet Commander in Charge, it is my duty and pleasure to announce — in recognition of his extraordinary performance, especially in applying target solutions and prioritizations during an ongoing battle, I herewith award you, Yusef, the Duchy's Silver Star for your gallantry. Moreover, as our last two kills were based on your solutions, you're entitled to wear two stars for these successful kills in battle."

This time, the applause came with approving cheers and

shouts that echoed through the ship.

Yusef looked down at the new decorations on his chest.

Mo slapped his shoulder. "Well done, Yusef! I always knew I had a good crew, but I had no clue how good you could be."

The merchant skipper turned to Haiki. "It takes some balls to enter a vented section in battle — hats off to our snipe!"

"What's a snipe?" Jona asked.

"A navy member who breathes oil and feeds on excess spare parts," Karim explained. "Military only, of course. Merchants can only afford stokers."

Haiki wore his award proudly, but when Gwen winked at him, he climbed down quickly.

Syreen waved at the audience. "Thank you all for your attention. Now — enjoy the party!"

Syreen noticed company and turned around. Captain Aziz had followed her to the hallway. "A word, please."

"Sure, Karim."

"Ruben and I had a little discussion before. We came to the conclusion you shouldn't show up in the Woo system. That wouldn't be good for us, and it would be far worse for you."

"I agree."

"In fact, better you should find your own route from here on. If your extraordinarily skilled pilot could prepare another fast jump solution for us, we'll surely get there unharmed. Kathmandu occasionally gets escort or patrol ship visits — pirates don't like that."

"We made a deal. I should guide you to Woo."

"Yes, and you kept that deal. You might have noticed — all of us were in a kind of desperate situation. Otherwise we wouldn't have considered such a dangerous run."

"You shouldn't tell me. It jeopardizes your negotiation base."

"Haha—yes, you're right. But we're not negotiating. In fact, you're not one to negotiate with. You're honest and straightforward, and your word is worth a star's weight in reaction mass. Which isn't quite what we earned on this trip, but you've put us—all of us—in the comfortable situation of polishing up our ships, affording a few empty jumps, and then picking a next contract to our liking. We're not extremely rich, but at least a kind of wealthy—for a freelance merchant, and that's your doing. Two reasons—and doing what we came for isn't one of them. Firstly, your jumps saved us a fortune on maintenance. Secondly, your choice of route earned us another fortune on extra deals. Again, all of us. That's why we decided to pay your fee for the last leg just for the route calculation."

Syreen considered declining, but she could sense he was serious—and determined not to be turned down. It seemed to be a question of honor. If she didn't want a fight, she had to agree.

"In that case, thank you."

He opened his mouth, paused, then took a deep breath. "I doubt any of the others feels different, but, well, that's their business. For my part, I can only say—I owe you. If there's anything in my power I can do for you, any time now or in the future, don't hesitate to ask."

He meant it.

"One day," she said.

They gazed at each other.

With a nod, she turned away.

CHAPTER FIFTY-FOUR

Yusef opened a line. "Folks, *Bumblebee* will leave you alone now. Have a safe journey to Woo."

Shiny Tin Can answered first. *"Hey, Yusef, it's just a last double-jump. No worries. Remember I promised you a beer."*

"Won't forget that, Simon."

One after another, the other skippers reported back with best wishes. They kept it short—had to keep it short in order not to waste Yusef's jump solution. Captain Palmer of *Veronica's Smile* just managed to slip his farewell in before the fifteen ships disappeared from Yusef's board—of course, with not even the slightest jitter.

"We're on our own now," he said. "Where to?"

"Appalahoo," Syreen answered.

"Okay." He called up the catalog and searched for the name. "Really? And I thought Backwater was remote."

"You'll like it there. It's a vacation spot."

He wasn't sure what to make of her grin, but he started calculations anyway.

"Nah." With disgust, Yusef discarded his fourth solution, and started another approach.

"Trouble?" Syreen asked.

"Not really. But this region's difficult to sail. Five-sigmas or worse everywhere. The sixes are hard to find, and sevens—well."

"Shall I have a look?"

"Please, yes. I tried."

184

She came over to his board and leaned across. He could see the hair on her arms, could smell her, could sense the warmth she radiated, but couldn't spare time to focus on any of those. He was too eager to see her working another navigation miracle.

With her first attempt, she arrived at almost the same solution he'd just wiped out. Three sixes and a five in between. Where would she find the better route?

She didn't even try. Instead, she called up the fine tuning and began to change parameters — a nudge here, a nick there, a secondary entry point — nothing extraordinary, just the fine adjustment he did with every other jump. The numbers got worse, even down to four-sigma.

"Hopeless," he said.

"Agreed. We don't need hope, we need a trick. Watch." She smiled and added another change.

There it was, as if it'd been there all the time, in plain sight, only he hadn't recognized it — a beautiful seven-seven-six-seven sequence. Why? Only because she had reduced a safety level by a margin hardly worth mentioning.

"Computers are stupid," she said. "They stubbornly stick to their rules. That safety level was set for a reason — but that reason doesn't apply to seven-sigma jumpers. Give it a little leeway, and it can see what we're seeing now. You expected to find it on this route, admit it. You picked the best, only the computer wouldn't show it to you."

"I'd never have found it."

"No, indeed not. Safety levels are there for a reason, and you're not supposed to fiddle with them. You knew where to look for the best route, and I knew how close you'd come — I knew there had to be a seven-sigma solution. Only because I already knew that did I dare to touch the safeties. I daresay only few pilots would have come as far as you. So don't worry."

185

"Thank you." He might have felt flattered, but that wasn't her way. She spoke the truth. "Oookay—should we do it, then?"

"Yes, go ahead. I'd like to recharge after the third, though, and make sure we have another jump solution ready, just in case."

Just in case we encounter an enemy warship, I know. I have a jump solution ready – that's what I did before I tried to find the long route.

"Okay. Crew, folks, prepare for double jump in ten."

CHAPTER FIFTY-FIVE

Yusef stared at his board, checked the readings, checked again. Ships as small as their *Bumblebee,* sleek and shining, but their transponder codes said *civil.* "What's that, by all ghosts in space?"

"Yachts," Syreen said. "Three private yachts and one liner."

"Here? Out in the middle of nowhere?"

"Appalahoo is a vacation spot, as I told you. People come here to enjoy nature—and go hunting."

"Hunting?"

"Shooting wild animals."

"Uh—I wasn't aware anyone could shoot animals for recreational purposes. Sounds wrong to me."

"It's frowned upon in the Duchy. I don't know about others, but I agree with you. People come here for the thrill—the local fauna is quite dangerous."

"Dangerous, like in a rogue place like Corfu?"

"Dangerous, like sailing your ship into a pirate's nest."

"Oh." He considered that. "I think I can do without a stroll around the place."

"Around the harbor, you're okay—daylight time."

"You know this place?"

"I did a stroll around the place before—at night, in the forest. Exciting."

"As exciting as dirtside Gattaca?"

"Yes, about like that. There's a minor difference—the Gattaca locals rape you, the Appalahoo locals eat you."

187

"I'm more and more in love with this place."

Finally, the call came.

"This is Appalahoo port authority. Unknown frigate, please state the purpose of your visit."

He glanced at Syreen. His skipper nodded. *As agreed.*

"Appalahoo, this is Duchy frigate *Bumblebee.* We came for a few spare parts, a drink and a breath of fresh air, and then we're on our way again."

Yusef turned to her. "They sound a bit reserved."

"We're a warship. That inevitably causes a little tension. But don't worry—they're okay."

Until their reply arrived, he could check the long-range scans. Nothing. What about the civil ships? They wouldn't dare to move now, until the situation was clarified.

"Bumblebee, you're welcome, but we regrettably do not offer shuttle services."

Yusef grinned. "Appalahoo, our skipper will take us down. Your landing field is large enough, and your mud isn't deep enough to swallow us."

He switched off. "That will give them something to think about."

Syreen grinned. "They haven't seen our ground force yet— I'm sure the girls will have their fun, too."

They waited for the next reply.

"Bumblebee, our records indicate no previous visit."

"Appalahoo, our ship hasn't been here before, only our skipper. She's eager to meet old acquaintances again."

Very gently, *Bumblebee* settled down on the muddy surface. Only when Syreen was sure the ship wouldn't move anymore did she release her grip around the stick.

"Settled," she announced. "Want to come along?"

"Someone must keep watch," Yusef said. "I'm the pilot. Haiki wants to have a look at our hull from outside, Mo will shop for parts, you take care of the authorities, and I have no business outside. So I'm the natural choice. Don't worry, I'm fine with that. I'll examine the safety level programming—I want to know how it works."

"That's okay. It never hurts to learn more about the programming your life may depend upon."

Yusef grinned, and she rose. "You have the bridge."

"I have the bridge. Aye, skipper."

Their way across the spacefield was as muddy as Syreen knew it would be. For a moment, she wondered how the passengers of the other shuttles had dealt with the surface while heading for the boardwalk between customs and bar, as she had learned from Captain Estoril.

Mo and twenty-three girls followed in her wake. Like her, they all walked barefoot.

"I'm glad for the warning," Mo said. "This is, uh, very basic."

"They're good at selling boots. Girls, if you want a forwine, that's on my bill, but for everything else, you'd better find another sponsor. This is no place for fancy shopping."

"You mentioned something like that before," Jona said. "You also said it'd be safe outside."

"Between ship and building, in daylight, yes. Otherwise, no. You look pretty tasty—not just to Mo, but to local predators, too. So, enjoy the mud and the boardwalk, but stay in sight. Gattaca was civilized."

The entertainer said nothing. Syreen could sense her mixed feelings—finally being allowed a free walk outside *Bumblebee's* confined space, but again not entirely free. That had to be hard.

"I'm sorry. If you'd like to see more of the backcountry, we can do a walk together. That'll be safe, too."

"No, it's okay. You didn't promise us a bed of roses."

Syreen smiled and walked on. Ahead, she could already sense the curiosity of several guards and two familiar minds. Both stepped out on the boardwalk when she came close.

"It can't be true," the white-bearded man said. "Syreen?"

"Hi, Rico. Nice to meet you again." She faced the other. "Joe? I'd like to check my crew and passengers through."

The official head of Appalahoo's port authority waved at Rico. "This is your place. I'd appreciate you providing me a few details for the records before you leave."

She nodded. "Mo will provide you with all necessary details later. May I invite you to a forwine first? We can't stay long, but I'm curious about your other guests."

"It's the season," the shopkeeper explained. "Hunters are coming. As always, they bring their guides, leaving at dusk, returning at dawn, spending money in my shop."

Syreen smiled and followed him across the boardwalk. He hadn't told her everything, that much she could sense. "That's the official line. What's different this year?"

"Ah, I can't tell you stories, right? Nah, it's different this season. You've seen the liner? Several vacationers are missing, their guides, too. Others won't dare to go outside."

"What did they expect?" Syreen asked. "They know it's a dangerous place, don't they?"

They'd reached the outer shop door. Rico waved her in, and went on, "It's one of the big ones. We hear nothing, see nothing, but in the morning, there's a footprint, some broken scrub—once, a gun, soaked in blood—such things."

Only one table was occupied. Three men in expensive outdoor gear, with toned bodies and dark-tanned skin, stared at their mugs of forwine. When they noticed the new arrivals, they turned to the door.

One hunter said, "I'd go. I don't fear big predators, but I need a guide, someone to point out hazards and lead me back. I was told I'd find a professional guide here. Are you?"

Syreen shook her head. "I'm a starship skipper, not a guide. Nor did I bring guides, sorry. However, one thing I can tell you—you should fear those big predators. This is their home."

"They're just big animals. We're the ones with the guns. The local authorities should do something about the situation."

"What situation? You want to go hunting—grab your gun and get out. You're the ones with the guns—what do you fear? You against them—the better one wins."

"Easy talk. Of all things, what would you space jockeys know about them?"

Rico chimed in. "Casey—bring the holo."

A mid-aged woman came around the counter and placed the well-known image on the table. "Here."

The hunters stared at it, and Syreen's girls crowded around them to catch a glimpse of it, too. Their gaze soon wandered to the huge sauroid head mounted to the wall to the counter's side.

"Yeah, it's the same head," Rico said. "The only one we ever saw—those beasts don't show themselves during the day."

"And the rider?" the first hunter asked. "Is that . . ."

"That's her," Rico said. "She's the only one ever to hunt such a beast down, and the only one ever to command the smaller ones."

"I thought you said the smaller ones are dangerous, too?" a second hunter asked.

"They are," Syreen said. "Especially when hunting together. You think you've got one, you aim—and then two others come at you from behind. That way, they could even take a big one down."

"And this?" He pointed at the holo.

"These were my team when I took the big one down, after

191

he failed to show me due respect."

"But how—I don't even see a gun."

"I had no gun. I didn't need one. I just convinced them to collaborate."

Syreen sensed his disbelief—it was so obvious that Rico picked it up, too.

Rico placed one hand on the hunter's shoulder. "Before you start arguments, check the head on the wall again. It's real, just like this holo."

The shopkeeper turned to her. "Find a seat anywhere, I'll join you. Casey, we need twenty-seven forwine—no, make that twenty-eight and get yourself one, too. I assume that's okay for you, Syreen?"

"Of course." One more on her bill wouldn't make a difference.

Amused, Syreen noticed several of her girls already making closer acquaintance with the three bored hunters. They no longer had to work as entertainers for their living—not while they were with her—but if some preferred to act in their chosen profession, who was she to object?

Plus, the three men were handsome indeed—and rich.

"I've never heard of a frigate going down to the surface," Rico said. "Of course, I'm no expert in warships."

"They're not meant to," Syreen said. "Only my engineer wanted to have a look at a minor hull breach from the outside, and rather than going through the hassle of extravehicular activity, and in absence of a nice, pressurized orbital dock, I brought my ship down to make it easier for him."

"A hull breach—you had a battle? Wait—what do you mean letting him have a look from the outside? Here, on our spacefield?"

She felt his alarm. Why? "Sure."

"You put up guards?"

"No—it's still bright daylight."

"That doesn't mean anything if you don't have a gun. It's the season."

That didn't tell her much, but his concern did. So she reached out with her senses for traces of predators in the close vicinity.

Indeed, there were a few, but not close enough to cause Haiki any trouble.

No need to take chances.

Leave, she told them and smiled at Rico. "Don't worry. We're safe."

After the third round of forwine, their host arrived at the subject Syreen was most interested in.

"Yours isn't the first warship visiting us, you know," Rico said.

"A patrol searching for pirates?"

"Nah—no pirate in his sane mind would waste his time here. Those yachts, and the liner, too, are licensed."

"They're bearing guns?"

"Yes—locked down while in orbit, but in principle, they're armed. With those very important brats—um, people, aboard, they wouldn't risk sailing unprotected."

He looked around, but his very important clients had disappeared together with some of the girls. The head of port authority had left, too.

"You call them warships?"

"Nah—they don't count as warships. It's just self-defense. You know, pirates could only profit from taking them prisoners hostage and asking for a ransom, not from shooting them down. And if their prospective victim can shoot back, they have nothing to gain. No, about a kilocycle ago, we had an entire battle group come through. Associated Planets, I think. They had a chat with Joe, and then they left. They were kind of rude, he said. I can only agree. Unlike you, they wouldn't grant a poor businessman a little income, not even by purchasing forwine."

"Rude." She smiled and tried to hide her worries. An entire battle group wouldn't do her frigate any good. She'd have to run, and running away wouldn't help her return to Klondike and her small crew there.

"Well," she said. "With a full battle group, they surely scared away any potential pirate from this sector. Makes travel safer for us, I'd say. Not that I'd fear pirates. They're simply a nuisance."

"They were asking for a woman. They had a good description of her. Due to cleanup activities, I didn't have your holo on the counter." He grinned. "Rude, as I said. I don't like to volunteer information to people who are not my customers."

Was there a hidden message? "I'm all for supporting independent business."

"Oh, please—I don't want your credits, except for the forwine. After all, you gave me my most valuable marketing instrument for free." Again, he pointed at the sauroid head. "Until recently, people came just to see it—and perhaps, to hunt another one. Now—well, it's different. I don't know what's happening."

"I can only guess, but if you had a lot of strangers with guns coming to your place shooting your people, what would you do?"

"Uh—I don't know."

"Organize defense? After someone showed you what cooperation is worth? I know these creatures. Don't judge them by their appearance. They're able to grasp the advantages of hunting in teams, and not just the small ones. For the first time since man came onto this planet, one of the leaders was taken down—he'd made a severe mistake."

"Which?"

"He failed to show me due respect. His fate may have

taught the others two things."

"Which would be?"

"One—not to underestimate strangers. Two—what cooperation is worth."

"You mean, they're cooperating against us?"

"Possible. Consider that, discuss it with Barney. Where is he, by the way?"

"Left us, a while after you did. Family business, he said." He made a sour face. "If they're cooperating like you said, are we safe inside here?"

Syreen shrugged. "Don't know. At least until they find out how to crack your doors. After that—be prepared for the worst. How well protected is your underground storage?"

Rico stared through her. "You could drop a shuttle on the lid without breaking the latter. But the side entrance—it's to keep people from stealing, not to withstand attacks. Like our doors up here, at best."

"In that case, I'd say you're safe for now, but not in the long run. You know I've felt those claws. If one of them makes up his mind, he'll cut your steel bars."

The shopkeeper shook his head. "How soon?"

"I have no clue."

"I should go on a little vacation—perhaps once this season's over. And considering how business is running, it'll be over soon. Thank you."

"How will you ship your merchandise out?"

"Not at all. I'll be lucky if I get a bunk on that liner. I've put some credits aside for a return ticket. Never good to bet on one card alone, you know? Poor Casey won't be as lucky." He focused on Syreen. "Can you take her along? I've seen the flock of kittens you brought—would you mind picking up one more?"

"You know the AP is after me."

"Yeah, but they're not after tearing you into pieces alive."

Yes, they are, at least something like that. She sighed. "I can't refuse. If she wants to come along."

"She's a good girl. Never tried to cheat me. Won't cause you trouble."

CHAPTER FIFTY-SIX

Once Syreen had exited Appalahoo's orbit, she allowed herself a sigh.

"Worried?" Yusef asked.

"Not as much as dirtside. We were a sitting duck. How much time does the AP need to bring a fleet over from Woo?"

He tapped his board. "Counting from the moment our merchants arrived there? If they didn't have to undock and sent the faster ships ahead, they'd already be here. A battle group with battle cruisers would arrive within the next ten-cycle."

"You already checked?"

"I had plenty of leisure time down there. I knew what to check the long-range scans for. I wanted to know myself. Now, where are we going next?"

"Klondike. An old mining planet, two more jumps out. Tricky jumps, so I'll prepare a first solution myself."

"Just in case."

"Just in case."

"Okay—but you'll let me try anyway?"

"Of course."

"Great. Thanks." Her pilot disappeared behind a wall of virtual screens.

She focused on her own calculations. Last time, she hadn't had the computer modifications needed for seven-sigma calculations, and last time, she hadn't been able to listen the way she could now. This time, her jumps should be much better.

197

"Skipper?"

"Hmmm?" Syreen looked up from her board. She had double-checked, triple-checked several solutions, but wasn't happy with their current progress yet. She had to be gentle with *Bumblebee*—frigates couldn't be procured easily.

"Did you really kill that beast? Mo told me of the head on the wall. Teeth as long as my arm?"

"Almost. No, I didn't kill that beast. I only commanded the team of smaller beasts that did it."

"Why?"

She had expected a *How,* and wasn't willing to explain her mind control abilities. Yusef's question was more welcome, but perhaps even more difficult to answer.

"We had a disagreement. The beast demanded respect—which I was willing to give—but refused to show me respect in return. I couldn't let that stand. I had to prove to myself that I can stand my ground." She sighed. "I didn't attack. I just went out into his territory. He came to kill me—not to eat me, but just to make his point. Instead, I made my point."

"That's something you're really good at—making your point. I had a chat with two of the shuttle pilots—Appalahoo has a reputation for squeezing credits out of its guests, spacefield occupation fees, precipitation collection fees, oh, yes, selling new boots to their guests—I wasn't contacted even once. Mo said the same—no one asked him for anything but a very reasonable basic harbor fee. You must have made a point to them before."

"Must've been when I brought that trophy, riding on the head of my team. Their guards never go out at night, only in armed teams during the day, for fear of encountering one of them. I came back with seven of the most dangerous predators on their planet, unarmed."

"Must've made them wet their pants."

"Almost. However, I didn't threaten them, didn't make

undue demands, didn't give them reason to complain. I only had asked for respect, and once they'd understood, we got along well. So—no grudges, no unpaid bills."

"Just respect."

"Exactly."

They still had a halfcycle to their jump when the alarms on the long-range sensors chimed.

Yusef only gave the data a quick glance, and then tapped his panel. "Skipper to the bridge. All hands, stand by for instructions."

His computer tried to interpret the aftereffects of the new arrivals' jump, compared it with its database, and offered details.

He took a deep breath. "All hands, general quarters. Passengers, get into your bunks, evac suits at hand, and buckle up."

Mo and Haiki followed right on Syreen's heels.

"Status?" Syreen asked and slid into her seat.

"AP ships—one battle cruiser, three light cruisers, four destroyers, one corvette. Destroyers are spreading out, all others except the corvette are decelerating toward the planet." He rechecked. "Update—the destroyers are on an interception course now and accelerating toward us."

"Smart," Syreen said. "They're not sending stingships. But they'll call us soon enough."

The first message originated from the battle cruiser, though.

"APS Bumblebee, *this is Admiral Santiago of APS Valkyrie. You will cut your acceleration within a centicycle after receiving this message and await further instructions, otherwise we will launch a kinetic strike against Appalahoo.*"

Mo opened his mouth.

Syreen shook her head. "Admiral Santiago, *Duchy frigate*

Bumblebee has received and recorded your message clearly. I will not surrender to the AP, whatever you do. Your actions will be on your conscience alone, and surely will be properly dealt with at your court-martial. However, before you do anything irreversible, consider how you'll explain to your superiors why you had to kill the CEOs of two of your navy's largest providers. In any case, the recording of your initial announcement will be made public."

She muted the line and glanced at her pilot. "Yusef, will they get us?"

He had expected the question. "Their destroyers might reach maximum shooting distance before we jump, and they might dare a chance shot before that."

"Okay. Time for another trick, eh?"

He wondered what she meant, but only until her next announcement.

"Crew, passengers, prepare for rough double jump in two."

Next, she pushed a jump solution to his board.

He checked it. *Five-sigma, from our current position to an uncharted destination in an unnamed pivot system — but surely a surprise for the AP.*

Her solution already contained the following jump to Klondike, too. Again to an uncharted arrival point, again only little better than five-sigma — why?

Yusef tweaked three parameters each — the ones he had found most helpful during his own calculations — and sent his solution back.

Syreen grinned. "Six-sigma it is, okay. Good job, Yusef."

Bumblebee didn't wait for Admiral Santiago's reply. With its jump field established, it entered hypercontinuum to cheat on the light speed barrier, dropped back within what felt like no time at all, and exposed itself to the light and gravity of Klondike's central star.

CHAPTER FIFTY-SEVEN

Yusef gazed at his board. *Escaped, but only barely. And now? We're stuck at the farthest point of known space, with a full battle fleet on our heels. It won't take them long to follow us, and what are we supposed to do then?*

His skipper was already on the radio again.

"Klondike port authority, this is Duchy frigate *Bumblebee,* Fleet Commander in Charge Syreen speaking. I'm here for a rendezvous with my fleet and must ask you not to interfere. Sorry for the inconvenience."

Rendezvous? Fleet? What's she talking about?

"*Raydancer,* this is Syreen. Crew, prepare for emergency takeoff and rendezvous by plan *Icarus.* Do not confirm, just get your ass off the planet within ten. I mean it."

Raydancer—*her corvette? Here? Oh, a frigate plus a corvette, now that's a* fleet.

"*Assiduous,* this is Syreen. Prepare to surface and to pick me up."

Another ship? She never mentioned that.

He held his breath when he saw her setting a new course— almost straight into the star, and accelerating. Would she do a swing-by at relativistic speed?

She gazed at him. "If they found out about Appalahoo, how likely is it they found out about Klondike, too?"

"I don't know," he said. *Poor answer.* "I take it you were here before. Did you mention your name to the authorities?"

"Sadly, I did. No one would have taken an unknown girl along—but as a star angel, I could travel."

201

"In that case, I'd say it isn't just likely but a certainty."

She sighed. "In that case, it's a certainty they'll follow me here, or worse, send one fleet each to Appalahoo and to Klondike. When could they arrive?"

He focused on the question. "Two more jumps—or they might have found a different route—a cycle or two after Santiago, perhaps."

"And if they're willing to lose a ship or two?"

What could a navy vessel do if driven beyond its construction limits? Anything. After he had learned about *Bumblebee's* safety levels, a ten to twenty percent gain wasn't out of the question. Considering Santiago's unexpectedly early arrival at Appalahoo . . .

"Any moment now, unless they're already here."

His skipper nodded. "So, anything between a moment and a cycle. Well, they'll be in for a surprise, too."

Syreen could sense her crew's tension. She had to do something about that. Yusef was already busy calculating jumps into unknown territory, but the others . . .

"Haiki, we'll soon be exposed to some extra heat. Cut down any aggregate that's not essential—we need air to breathe, and that's it."

"The hull breach won't take that strain well."

"Can you do something to improve it? Seal off the compartment behind it or whatever, but we must do that dive."

"I'll find a solution."

"Thanks. Mo—the girls. Tell them we'll shut down the plumbing soon. They can have a last leak now, in turns, and then get into their suits. Have your suit ready, too."

"Sure. What else can I tell them?"

"You can promise them better accommodation soon, as we'll change ships. And an end to this running-away."

He raised an eyebrow. "Here? I mean, okay, it's a cul-desac, so it's a natural dead end for our run, too, but I'd expected something more glorious."

"You'll get plenty of glorious." Before she could explain, the chimes rang. *Bumblebee's* long-range sensors had picked up the aftershock of multiple jumps. The AP fleet had arrived.

Yusef quickly prepared an overview for her, and it wasn't looking good. The AP had sent not one, but three more battle groups after her, totaling three battle cruisers, nine light cruisers, nineteen destroyers, plus all the stingships and missiles their large units would carry.

The destroyers dashed away, the light cruisers lined up and hid behind their big tanks, and not long after that, the expected message came.

"*AP frigate* Bumblebee, *cut your engines. This is Admiral Cortez of AP battle cruiser* Vindicator. *I will promise your crew and guests fair treatment if you surrender now. You cannot escape anyway.*"

From what Yusef could see, the admiral was right. Cortez' own battle group took up the pursuit, the second was decelerating rapidly, probably to block their own arrival point, and the third was heading for the primary departure point. Their destroyers were spreading out to intercept *Bumblebee* on any of the probable swing-by courses she could take if she tried to run.

"We're not here to escape," Syreen said to her pilot. "We're here to stand our ground and fight."

"With this frigate?"

"Of course not. Check your panels. *Assiduous* will surface from the photosphere any moment now."

She could actually sense her partner already, although they hadn't even passed the planet's orbit around the star.

You need to know what you're looking for. The living ship didn't give its presence away by common electromagnetic radiation. Aside from visuals, only the gravitational anomaly its drive produced could be spotted by well-calibrated sensors.

For her crew's and passengers' benefit, she highlighted the respective data and allowed the computer to create a visual model.

Yusef gasped.

Assiduous was looking good indeed. No longer the dried-out, darkened relic of ages long past, the fully charged ship was now gleaming with power.

She activated the internal communication system. "Folks, have you ever heard of the *Forgotten People?* It's time to remember. This is *Assiduous,* a living ship — *my* living ship."

To be continued . . .

YOU MAY ALSO ENJOY THE FOLLOWING FROM EXTASY BOOKS INC:

Time of Wisdom
Valerie J. Long

Excerpt

Mo stared at the green-golden U-shape on his board.

"This is Assiduous, a living ship—my living ship." Syreen's last line was on replay in his mind.

He hadn't heard of Forgotten People, or if he had, he didn't remember, he'd accepted her claim to the title Navigator as a quirk—although she indeed was the best navigator ever—but he had heard of living ships . . . in fairytales.

"How did you know it's here?"

Klondike certainly wasn't the first place where he'd expect to find materialized old lore—a remote place, at the outskirts of known space, but still a place with regular traffic.

"I brought Assiduous here. He needed time to recover—in a safe place, where the AP wouldn't find him."

"He. Okay. And how did you know how to fly such a ship?"

"He taught me what I didn't know already, but I'm a Navigator, remember?"

"You mentioned that often enough, but what does it really

mean?"

"It means I'm born to fly living ships. Only females of the People can integrate with them and take control."

"I don't get it." His mind stubbornly refused to draw conclusions from her statements. It can't be.

"Mo, I'm no human. I'm a descendant of an ancient race few of your people remember, and those who do call us the Forgotten People. Sadly, Assiduous is one of the only two connections to my past I have. I was raised by Duchy Navy as an orphan—a foundling, dropped on a busy orbital station. I never met my parents. I have no one to ask about my legacy."

"What is the other connection?"

"The head of Associated Planets Navy. He's of the People, too. He wants me—he needs me to control Assiduous, because he could never do it himself."

"He couldn't? Why?"

"Assiduous won't accept a male. It's impossible. You'll see."

Yusef listened. Everything she said sounded odd—but in an odd way, it made sense. It explained what she did—finding new routes, calculating seven-sigma jumps, dodging pulse shots, shooting more precisely than anyone else, or going dirtside with a spaceship—and left room for even more miracles.

He only couldn't imagine what kind of miracle they'd need to fend off three battle cruisers, nine light cruisers, nineteen destroyers, and a yet unknown number of stingships and missiles.

He'd grown fond of the ship they'd arrived with. Bumblebee was a swift and tough little warship, everything a solo pilot could ask for, but in the upcoming battle she was outclassed and outnumbered. There was no way for a single frigate to survive.

Their enemy surely had come to the same assessment. While his flagship was trying to catch up and his smaller units were cutting off their potential escape routes, he signaled again.

"APS Bumblebee, this is Admiral Cortez of APS Vindicator. You failed to follow my instructions. Unless you surrender instantly, I'm no longer in a position to give you quarter."

This time, Syreen decided to answer. "Admiral Cortez, unfortunately I can't give you what you want. However, should you at least be willing to formally declare war, I'll be ready to accept your capitulation any time. Just don't wait too long."

No way, Yusef thought. They didn't come in numbers to say hi and bye. Too bad for them—they didn't see her fight. Or—wait.

"Skipper?"

"What is it, Yusef?"

"What if they got data from our convoy, and know you can dodge pulse shots?"

"That won't help them."

Syreen kept her attention on the board. Until we reach Assiduous, we're vulnerable. They won't be able to catch up, but I'd credit them for trying anything else. Like . . .

She quickly entered a few parameters, rechecked them, and hit the button.

Bumblebee's two aft lasers fired, three times each, with reduced power. Six explosions indicated the successful elimination of six long-range missiles that had almost reached their frigate.

"Nice try," she said. "Okay, Admiral Cortez, you're playing your game well. Let's see how you deal with my next move."

"What are you up to?" Yusef asked. "You think you can hit him across this distance?"

"I could, but it would only be a tickle—or I could ruin our guns and burn a hole through his armor. Surely his repair crews would appreciate the drill. No. I didn't want to show him my tricks, but we need time for boarding Assiduous, and if he's willing to spend some more of his missiles, he might get at us at the very worst moment. No, I'll have to do something unconventional." Which she was entering right this moment.

"More unconventional than scoring impossible hits? I'm curious."

"In that case, check this out." She pushed her new solution over to his board.

Yusef glanced at it. "Seriously? No, of course you are. Again, you make the impossible possible. I wouldn't have thought of that."

"Neither did Cortez." She frowned and pulled her stick. Bumblebee changed course. "But he's learning fast—too fast to my taste."

"What was that?"

"Pulse shots from his destroyers. They must have used a kind of triangulation algorithm, or whatever it's called for nineteen instead of three angles, to shoot at us. Not precise enough to hit, and in any case, their shots couldn't have killed us, but—crap."

She pulled again and dodged another bouquet of nineteen well-aimed shots. "Yes, he knows—Crew, prepare for jump now."

Bumblebee jumped.

ABOUT THE AUTHOR

I am Valerie J. Long, born in 1963. I live and work in Germany as an IT project manager. I like role playing games, and I like putting my ideas on paper. I like all kinds of Science Fiction and Fantasy, I like music, and I like making you bite your nails off.